"I sank Atlantis," Render explained, "personally.

"It was about three years ago. And God! it was lovely! It was all ivory towers and silver balconies. There were bridges of opal, and crimson pennants and a milk-white river flowing between lemon-colored banks. There were jade steeples, and trees as old as the world tickling the bellies of clouds, and ships in the great sea-harbor of Xanadu, as delicately constructed as musical instruments, all swaying with the tides. The twelve princes of the realm held court in the dozen-pillared Colosseum of the Zodiac, to listen to a Greek tenor sax play at sunset.

"The Greek, of course, was a patient of mine—paranoiac. The etiology of the thing is rather complicated, but that's what I wandered into inside his mind. I gave him free rein for awhile, and in the end I had to split Atlantis in half and sink it full fathom five. I still see him periodically, but he is no longer the last descendant of the greatest minstrel of Atlantis. He's just a fine, late-twentieth-century saxman.

"Sometimes though, as I look back on the apocalypse I worked within his vision of grandeur, I experience a fleeting sense of lost beauty—because, for a single moment, his abnormally intense feelings were my feelings, and he felt that his dream was the most beautiful thing in the world."

THE TOR DOUBLE NOVELS

A Meeting with Medusa by Arthur C. Clarke/*Green Mars* by Kim Stanley Robinson

Hardfought by Greg Bear/*Cascade Point* by Timothy Zahn

Born with the Dead by Robert Silverberg/*The Saliva Tree* by Brian W. Aldiss

No Truce with Kings by Poul Anderson/*Ship of Shadows* by Fritz Leiber

Enemy Mine by Barry B. Longyear/*Another Orphan* by John Kessel

Screwtop by Vonda N. McIntyre/*The Girl Who Was Plugged In* by James Tiptree, Jr.

The Nemesis from Terra by Leigh Brackett/*Battle for the Stars* by Edmond Hamilton

The Ugly Little Boy by Isaac Asimov/*The [Widget], The [Wadget], and Boff* by Theodore Sturgeon

Sailing to Byzantium by Robert Silverberg/*Seven American Nights* by Gene Wolfe

Houston, Houston, Do You Read? by James Tiptree, Jr./*Souls* by Joanna Russ

*The Blind Geometer by Kim Stanley Robinson/*The New Atlantis* by Ursula K. Le Guin

*forthcoming

ROGER ZELAZNY
HE WHO SHAPES

A TOM DOHERTY ASSOCIATES BOOK
NEW YORK

This is a work of fiction. All the characters and events portrayed in this book are fictitious, and any resemblance to real people or events is purely coincidental.

HE WHO SHAPES

Copyright © 1965 by Ziff-Davis Publishing Co., Inc.; copyright © 1989 by The Amber Corporation.

All rights reserved, including the right to reproduce this book or portions thereof in any form.

A TOR Book
Published by Tom Doherty Associates, Inc.
49 West 24 Street
New York, NY 10010

Cover art by Wayne Barlowe

ISBN: 0-812-55879-0   Can. ISBN: 0-812-50266-3

First edition: September 1989

Printed in the United States of America

0 9 8 7 6 5 4 3 2 1

I

Lovely as it was, with the blood and all, Render could sense that it was about to end.

Therefore, each microsecond would be better off as a minute, he decided—and perhaps the temperature should be increased . . . Somewhere, just at the periphery of everything, the darkness halted its constriction.

Something, like a crescendo of subliminal thunders, was arrested at one raging note. That note was a distillate of shame and pain, and fear.

The Forum was stifling.

Caesar cowered outside the frantic circle. His forearm covered his eyes but it could not stop the seeing, not this time.

The senators had no faces and their garments were spattered with blood. All their voices were like the cries of birds. With an inhuman frenzy they plunged their daggers into the fallen figure.

All, that is, but Render.

The pool of blood in which he stood continued to widen. His arm seemed to be rising and falling with a mechanical regularity and his throat might have been shaping bird-cries, but he was simultaneously apart from and a part of the scene.

For he was Render, the Shaper.

Crouched, anguished and envious, Caesar wailed his protests.

"You have slain him! You have murdered Marcus Antonius—a blameless, useless fellow!"

Render turned to him, and the dagger in his hand was quite enormous and quite gory.

"Aye," said he.

The blade moved from side to side. Caesar, fascinated by the sharpened steel, swayed to the same rhythm.

"Why?" he cried. "Why?"

"Because," answered Render, "he was a far nobler Roman than yourself."

"You lie! It is not so!"

Render shrugged and returned to the stabbing.

"It is not true!" screamed Caesar. "Not true!"

Render turned to him again and waved the dagger. Puppetlike, Caesar mimicked the pendulum of the blade.

"Not true?" smiled Render. "And who are you to question an assassination such as this? You are no one! You detract from the dignity of this occasion! Begone!"

Jerkily, the pink-faced man rose to his feet, his hair half-wispy, half-wetplastered, a disarray of cotton. He turned, moved away; and as he walked, he looked back over his shoulder.

He had moved far from the circle of assassins, but the scene did not diminish in size. It retained an electric clarity. It made him feel even further removed, ever more alone and apart.

Render rounded a previously unnoticed corner and stood before him, a blind beggar.

Caesar grasped the front of his garment.

"Have you an ill omen for me this day?"

"Beware!" jeered Render.

"Yes! Yes!" cried Caesar. " 'Beware!' That is good! Beware what?"

"The ides—"

"Yes? The ides—"

"—of October."

He released the garment.

"What is that you say? What is October?"

"A month."

"You lie! There is no month of Octember!"

"And that is the date noble Caesar need fear—the non-existent time, the never-to-be-calendared occasion."

Render vanished around another sudden corner.

"Wait! Come back!"

Render laughed, and the Forum laughed with him. The bird-cries became a chorus of inhuman jeers.

"You mock me!" wept Caesar.

The Forum was an oven, and the perspiration formed like a glassy mask over Caesar's narrow forehead, sharp nose, chinless jaw.

"I want to be assassinated too!" he sobbed. "It isn't fair!"

And Render tore the Forum and the senators and the grinning corpse of Antony to pieces and stuffed them into a black sack—with the unseen movement of a single finger—and last of all went Caesar.

Charles Render sat before the ninety white buttons and the two red ones, not really looking at any of them. His right arm moved in its soundless sling, across the lap-level surface of the console—pushing some of the buttons, skipping over others, moving on, retracing its path to press the next in the order of the Recall Series.

Sensations throttled, emotions reduced to nothing, Representative Erikson knew the oblivion of the womb.

There was a soft click.

Render's hand had glided to the end of the bottom row of buttons. An act of conscious intent—will, if you like—was required to push the red button.

Render freed his arm and lifted off his crown of Medusa-hair leads and microminiature circuitry. He slid from behind his desk-couch and raised the hood. He walked to the window and transpared it, fingering forth a cigarette.

One minute in the ro-womb, he decided. *No more. This is a crucial one. . . . Hope it doesn't snow till later—those clouds look mean. . . .*

It was smooth yellow trellises and high towers, glassy

and gray, all smouldering into evening under a shale-colored sky; the city was squared volcanic islands, glowing in the end-of-day light, rumbling deep down under the earth; it was fat, incessant rivers of traffic, rushing.

Render turned away from the window and approached the great egg that lay beside his desk, smooth and glittering. It threw back a reflection that smashed all aquilinity from his nose, turned his eyes to gray saucers, transformed his hair into a light-streaked sky-line; his reddish necktie became the wide tongue of a ghoul.

He smiled, reached across the desk. He pressed the second red button.

With a sigh, the egg lost its dazzling opacity and a horizontal crack appeared about its middle. Through the now-transparent shell, Render could see Erikson grimacing, squeezing his eyes tight, fighting against a return to consciousness and the thing it would contain. The upper half of the egg rose vertical to the base, exposing him knobby and pink on half-shell. When his eyes opened he did not look at Render. He rose to his feet and began dressing. Render used this time to check the ro-womb.

He leaned back across his desk and pressed the buttons: temperature control, full range, *check*; exotic sounds—he raised the earphone—*check*, on bells, on buzzes, on violin notes and whistles, on squeals and moans, on traffic noises and the sound of surf; *check*, on the feedback circuit—holding the patient's own voice, trapped earlier in analysis; *check*, on the sound blanket, the moisture spray, the odor banks; *check*, on the couch agitator and the colored lights, the taste stimulants . . .

Render closed the egg and shut off its power. He pushed the unit into the closet, palmed shut the door. The tapes had registered a valid sequence.

"Sit down," he directed Erikson.

The man did so, fidgeting with his collar.

"You have full recall," said Render, "so there is no need for me to summarize what occurred. Nothing can be hidden from me. I was there."

Erikson nodded.

"The significance of the episode should be apparent to you."

Erikson nodded again, finally finding his voice. "But was it valid?" he asked. "I mean, you constructed the dream and you controlled it, all the way. I didn't really *dream* it—in the way I would normally dream. Your ability to make things happen stacks the deck for whatever you're going to say—doesn't it?"

Render shook his head slowly, flicked an ash into the southern hemisphere of his globe-made-ashtray, and met Erikson's eyes.

"It is true that I supplied the format and modified the forms. You, however, filled them with an emotional significance, promoted them to the status of symbols corresponding to your problem. If the dream was not a valid analogue it would not have provoked the reactions it did. It would have been devoid of the anxiety-patterns which were registered on the tapes.

"You have been in analysis for many months now," he continued, "and everything I have learned thus far serves to convince me that your fears of assassination are without any basis in fact."

Erikson glared.

"Then why the hell do I have them?"

"Because," said Render, "you would like very much to be the subject of an assassination."

Erikson smiled then, his composure beginning to return.

"I assure you, doctor, I have never contemplated suicide, nor have I any desire to stop living."

He produced a cigar and applied a flame to it. His hand shook.

"When you came to me this summer," said Render,

"you stated that you were in fear of an attempt on your life. You were quite vague as to why anyone should want to kill you—"

"My position! You can't be a Representative as long as I have and make no enemies!"

"Yet," replied Render, "it appears that you have managed it. When you permitted me to discuss this with your detectives I was informed that they could unearth nothing to indicate that your fears might have any real foundation. Nothing."

"They haven't looked far enough—or in the right places. They'll turn up something."

"I'm afraid not."

"Why?"

"Because, I repeat, your feelings are without any objective basis.—Be honest with me. Have you any information whatsoever indicating that someone hates you enough to want to kill you?"

"I receive many threatening letters. . . ."

"As do all Representatives—and all of those directed to you during the past year have been investigated and found to be the work of cranks. Can you offer me *one* piece of evidence to substantiate your claims?"

Erikson studied the tip of his cigar.

"I came to you on the advice of a colleague," he said, "came to you to have you poke around inside my mind to find me something of that sort, to give my detectives something to work with. —Someone I've injured severely perhaps—or some damaging piece of legislation I've dealt with . . ."

"—And I found nothing," said Render, "nothing, that is, but the cause of your discontent. Now, of course, you are afraid to hear it, and you are attempting to divert me from explaining my diagnosis—"

"I am not!"

"Then listen. You can comment afterwards if you want, but you've poked and dawdled around here for months, unwilling to accept what I presented to you in a dozen different forms. Now I am going to tell you out-right what it is, and you can do what you want about it."

"Fine."

"First," he said, "you would like very much to have an enemy or enemies—"

"Ridiculous!"

"—Because it is the only alternative to having friends—"

"I have lots of friends!"

"—Because nobody wants to be completely ignored, to be an object for whom no one has really strong feelings. Hatred and love are the ultimate forms of human regard. Lacking one, and unable to achieve it, you sought the other. You wanted it so badly that you succeeded in convincing yourself it existed. But there is always a psychic pricetag on these things. Answering a genuine emotional need with a body of desire-surrogates does not produce real satisfaction, but anxie-ty, discomfort—because in these matters the psyche should be an open system. You did not seek outside yourself for human regard. You were closed off. You created that which you needed from the stuff of your own being. You are a man very much in need of strong relationships with other people."

"Manure!"

"Take it or leave it," said Render. "I suggest you take it."

"I've been paying you for half a year to help find out who wants to kill me. Now you sit there and tell me I made the whole thing up to satisfy a desire to have someone hate me."

"Hate you, or love you. That's right."

"It's absurd! I meet so many people that I carry a pocket recorder and a lapel-camera, just so I can recall them all. . . ."

"Meeting quantities of people is hardly what I was speaking of.—Tell me, *did* that dream sequence have a strong meaning for you?"

Erikson was silent for several tickings of the huge wallclock.

"Yes," he finally conceded, "it did. But your interpretation of the matter is still absurd. Granting though, just for the sake of argument, that what you say is correct—what would I do to get out of this bind?"

Render leaned back in his chair.

"Rechannel the energies that went into producing the thing. Meet some people as yourself, Joe Erikson, rather than Representative Erikson. Take up something you can do with other people—something non-political, and perhaps somewhat competitive—and make some real friends or enemies, preferably the former. I've encouraged you to do this all along."

"Then tell me something else."

"Gladly."

"Assuming you *are* right, why is it that I am neither liked nor hated, and never have been? I have a responsible position in the Legislature. I meet people all the time. Why am I so neutral a—thing?"

Highly familiar now with Erikson's career, Render had to push aside his true thoughts on the matter, as they were of no operational value. He wanted to cite him Dante's observations concerning the trimmers—those souls who, denied heaven for their lack of virtue, were also denied entrance to hell for a lack of significant vices—in short, the ones who trimmed their sails to move them with every wind of the times, who lacked direction, who were not really concerned toward which ports they were pushed. Such was Erikson's long and colorless career of migrant loyalties, of political reversals.

Render said:

"More and more people find themselves in such circumstances these days. It is due largely to the increasing complexity of society and the depersonalization of the individual into a sociometric unit. Even the act of cathecting toward other persons has grown more forced as a result. There are so many of us these days."

Erikson nodded, and Render smiled inwardly.

Sometimes the gruff line, and then the lecture . . .

"I've got the feeling you could be right," said Erikson. "Sometimes I *do* feel like what you described—a unit, something depersonalized. . . ."

Render glanced at the clock.

"What you choose to do about it from here is, of course, your own decision to make. I think you'd be wasting your time to remain in analysis any longer. We are now both aware of the cause of your complaint. I can't take you by the hand and show you how to lead your life. I can indicate, I can commiserate—but no more deep probing. Make an appointment as soon as you feel a need to discuss your activities and relate them to my diagnosis."

"I will," nodded Erikson, "and—damn that dream! It got to me. You can make them seem as vivid as waking life—more vivid. . . . It may be a long while before I can forget it."

"I hope so."

"Okay, doctor." He rose to his feet, extended a hand. "I'll probably be back in a couple weeks. I'll give this socializing a fair try." He grinned at the word he normally frowned upon. "In fact, I'll start now. May I buy you a drink around the corner, downstairs?"

Render met the moist palm which seemed as weary of the performance as a lead actor in too successful a play. He felt almost sorry as he said, "Thank you, but I have an engagement."

Render helped him on with his coat then, handed him his hat, saw him to the door.

"Well, good night."

"Good night."

As the door closed soundlessly behind him, Render re-crossed the dark Astrakhan to his mahogany fortress and flipped his cigarette into the southern hemisphere. He leaned back in his chair, hands behind his head, eyes closed.

"Of course it was more real than life," he informed no one in particular. "I shaped it."

Smiling, he reviewed the dream sequence step by step, wishing some of his former instructors could have witnessed it. It had been well-constructed and powerfully executed, as well as being precisely appropriate for the case at hand. But then, he was Render, the Shaper—one of the two hundred or so special analysts whose own psychic makeup permitted them to enter into neurotic patterns without carrying away more than an esthetic gratification from the mimesis of aberrance—a Sane Hatter.

Render stirred his recollections. He had been analyzed himself, analyzed and passed upon as a granite-willed, ultra-stable outsider—tough enough to weather the basilisk gaze of a fixation, walk unscathed amidst the chimaerae of perversions, force dark Mother Medusa to close her eyes before the caduceus of his art. His own analysis had not been difficult. Nine years before (it seemed much longer) he had suffered a willing injection of Novocain into the most painful area of his spirit. It was after the auto wreck, after the death of Ruth, and of Miranda, their daughter, that he had begun to feel detached. Perhaps he did not want to recover certain empathies; perhaps his own world was now based upon a certain rigidity of feeling. If this was true, he was wise enough in the ways of the mind to realize it, and perhaps he had decided that such a world had its own compensations.

His son Peter was now ten years old. He was attending a school of quality, and he penned his father a letter every week. The letters were becoming progressively literate, showing signs of a precociousness of which Render could not but approve. He would take the boy with him to Europe in the summer.

As for Jill—Jill DeVille (what a luscious, ridiculous name!—he loved her for it)—she was growing, if anything, more interesting to him. (He wondered if this was an indication of early middle age.) He was vastly taken by her unmusical nasal voice, her sudden interest in architecture, her concern with the unremovable mole on the right side of her otherwise well-designed nose. He should really call her immediately and go in search of a new restaurant. For some reason though, he did not feel like it.

It had been several weeks since he had visited his club, The Partridge and Scalpel, and he felt a strong desire to eat from an oaken table, alone, in the split-level dining room with the three fireplaces, beneath the artificial torches and the boars' heads like gin ads. So he pushed his perforated membership card into the phone-slot on his desk and there were two buzzes behind the voice-screen.

"Hello, Partridge and Scalpel," said the voice. "May I help you?"

"Charles Render," he said. "I'd like a table in about half an hour."

"How many will there be?"

"Just me."

"Very good, sir. Half an hour, then.—That's 'Render'?—R-e-n-d-e-r?"

"Right."

"Thank you."

He broke the connection and rose from his desk. Outside, the day had vanished.

The monoliths and the towers gave forth their own light now. A soft snow, like sugar, was sifting down through the shadows and transforming itself into beads on the windowpane.

Render shrugged into his overcoat, turned off the lights, locked the inner office. There was a note on Mrs. Hedges' blotter.

Miss DeVille called, it said.

He crumpled the note and tossed it into the waste-chute. He would call her tomorrow and say he had been working until late on his lecture.

He switched off the final light, clapped his hat onto his head, and passed through the outer door, locking it as

he went. The drop took him to the sub-subcellar where
his auto was parked.

It was chilly in the sub-sub, and his footsteps seemed
loud on the concrete as he passed among the parked
vehicles. Beneath the glare of the naked lights, his S-7
Spinner was a sleek gray cocoon from which it seemed
turbulent wings might at any moment emerge. The
double row of antennae which fanned forward from the
slope of its hood added to this feeling. Render thumbed
open the door.

He touched the ignition and there was the sound of a
lone bee awakening in a great hive. The door swung
soundlessly shut as he raised the steering wheel and
locked it into place. He spun up the spiral ramp and
came to a rolling stop before the big overhead.

As the door rattled upward he lighted his destination
screen and turned the knob that shifted the broadcast
map.—Left to right, top to bottom, section by section
he shifted it, until he located the portion of Carnegie
Avenue he desired. He punched out its coordinates and
lowered the wheel. The car switched over to monitor
and moved out onto the highway marginal. Render lit a
cigarette.

Pushing his seat back into the centerspace, he left all
the windows transparent. It was pleasant to half-recline
and watch the oncoming cars drift past him like swarms
of fireflies. He pushed his hat back on his head and
stared upward.

He could remember a time when he had loved snow,
when it had reminded him of novels by Thomas Mann
and music by Scandinavian composers. In his mind
now, though, there was another element from which it
could never be wholly dissociated. He could visualize so
clearly the eddies of milk-white coldness that swirled
about his old manual-steer auto, flowing into its fire-
charred interior to rewhiten that which had been black-
ened; so clearly—as though he had walked toward it

across a chalky lakebottom—it, the sunken wreck, and he, the diver—unable to open his mouth to speak, for fear of drowning; and he knew, whenever he looked upon falling snow, that somewhere skulls were whitening. But nine years had washed away much of the pain, and he also knew that the night was lovely.

He was sped along the wide, wide roads, shot across high bridges, their surfaces slick and gleaming beneath his lights, was woven through frantic cloverleafs and plunged into a tunnel whose dimly glowing walls blurred by him like a mirage. Finally, he switched the windows to opaque and closed his eyes.

He could not remember whether he had dozed for a moment or not, which meant he probably had. He felt the car slowing, and he moved the seat forward and turned on the windows again. Almost simultaneously, the cutoff buzzer sounded. He raised the steering wheel and pulled into the parking dome, stepped out onto the ramp, and left the car to the parking unit, receiving his ticket from that box-headed robot which took its solemn revenge on mankind by sticking forth a cardboard tongue at everyone it served.

As always, the noises were as subdued as the lighting. The place seemed to absorb sound and convert it into warmth, to lull the tongue with aromas strong enough to be tasted, to hypnotize the ear with the vivid crackle of the triple hearths.

Render was pleased to see that his favorite table, in the corner off to the right of the smaller fireplace, had been held for him. He knew the menu from memory, but he studied it with zeal as he sipped a Manhattan and worked up an order to match his appetite. Shaping sessions always left him ravenously hungry.

"Doctor Render . . . ?"

"Yes?" He looked up.

"Doctor Shallot would like to speak with you," said the waiter.

"I don't know anyone named Shallot," he said. "Are you sure he doesn't want Bender? He's a surgeon from Metro who sometimes eats here. . . ."

The waiter shook his head.

"No, sir—'Render.' See here?" He extended a three-by-five card on which Render's full name was typed in capital letters. "Doctor Shallot has dined here nearly every night for the past two weeks," he explained, "and on each occasion has asked to be notified if you came in."

"Hm?" mused Render. "That's odd. Why didn't he just call me at my office?"

The waiter smiled and made a vague gesture.

"Well, tell him to come on over," he said, gulping his Manhattan, "and bring me another of these."

"Unfortunately, Doctor Shallot is blind," explained the waiter. "It would be easier if you—"

"All right, sure." Render stood up, relinquishing his favorite table with a strong premonition that he would not be returning to it that evening.

"Lead on."

They threaded their way among the diners, heading up to the next level. A familiar face said "hello" from a table set back against the wall, and Render nodded a greeting to a former seminar pupil whose name was Jurgens or Jirkans or something like that.

He moved on, into the smaller dining room wherein only two tables were occupied. No, three. There was one set in the corner at the far end of the darkened bar, partly masked by an ancient suit of armor. The waiter was heading him in that direction.

They stopped before the table and Render stared down into the darkened glasses that had tilted upward as they approached. Doctor Shallot was a woman, somewhere in the vicinity of her early thirties. Her low bronze bangs did not fully conceal the spot of silver which she wore on her forehead like a caste-mark. Render inhaled, and her head jerked slightly as the tip of his cigarette flared. She appeared to be staring straight up into his eyes. It was an uncomfortable feeling, even knowing that all she could distinguish of him was that which her minute photo-electric cell transmitted to her visual cortex over the hair-fine wire implants attached to that oscillator-convertor: in short, the glow of his cigarette.

"Doctor Shallot, this is Doctor Render," the waiter was saying.

"Good evening," said Render.

"Good evening," she said. "My name is Eileen and I've wanted very badly to meet you." He thought he detected a slight quaver in her voice. "Will you join me for dinner?"

- "My pleasure," he acknowledged, and the waiter drew out the chair.

Render sat down, noting that the woman across from him already had a drink. He reminded the waiter of his second Manhattan.

"Have you ordered yet?" he inquired.

"No."

". . . And two menus—" he started to say, then bit his tongue.

"Only one," she smiled.

"Make it none," he amended, and recited the menu. They ordered. Then:

"Do you always do that?"

"What?"

"Carry menus in your head."

"Only a few," he said, "for awkward occasions. What was it you wanted to see—talk to me about?"

"You're a neuroparticipant therapist," she stated, "a Shaper."

"And you are—?"

"—a resident in psychiatry at State Psych. I have a year remaining."

"You knew Sam Riscomb then."

"Yes, he helped me get my appointment. He was my adviser."

"He was a very good friend of mine. We studied

together at Menninger."

She nodded.

"I'd often heard him speak of you—that's one of the reasons I wanted to meet you. He's responsible for encouraging me to go ahead with my plans, despite my handicap."

Render stared at her. She was wearing a dark green dress which appeared to be made of velvet. About three inches to the left of the bodice was a pin which might have been gold. It displayed a red stone which could have been a ruby, around which the outline of a goblet was cast. Or was it really two profiles that were outlined, staring through the stone at one another? It seemed vaguely familiar to him, but he could not place it at the moment. It glittered expensively in the dim light.

Render accepted his drink from the waiter.

"I want to become a neuroparticipant therapist," she told him.

And if she had possessed vision Render would have thought she was staring at him, hoping for some response in his expression. He could not quite calculate what she wanted him to say.

"I commend your choice," he said, "and I respect your ambition." He tried to put his smile into his voice. "It is not an easy thing, of course, not all of the requirements being academic ones."

"I know," she said. "But then, I have been blind since birth and it was not an easy thing to come this far."

"Since birth?" he repeated. "I thought you might have lost your sight recently. You did your undergrad work then, and went on through med school without eyes. . . . That's—rather impressive."

"Thank you," she said, "but it isn't. Not really. I heard about the first neuroparticipants—Bartelmetz and the rest—when I was a child, and I decided then that I wanted to be one. My life ever since has been governed by that desire."

"What did you do in the labs?" he inquired. "—Not being able to see a specimen, look through a microscope . . . ? Or all that reading?"

"I hired people to read my assignments to me. I taped everything. The school understood that I wanted to go into psychiatry and they permitted a special arrangement for labs. I've been guided through the dissection of cadavers by lab assistants, and I've had everything described to me. I can tell things by touch . . . and I have a memory like yours with the menu," she smiled. "'The quality of psychoparticipation phenomena can only be gauged by the therapist himself, at that moment outside of time and space as we normally know it, when he stands in the midst of a world erected from the stuff of another man's dreams, recognizes there the non-Euclidian architecture of aberrance, and then takes his patient by the hand and tours the landscape. . . . If he can lead him back to the common earth, then his judgments were sound, his actions valid.'"

"From *Why No Psychometrics in This Place*," reflected Render.

"—by Charles Render, M.D."

"Our dinner is already moving in this direction," he noted, picking up his drink as the speed-cooked meal was pushed toward them in the kitchen-buoy.

"That's one of the reasons I wanted to meet you," she continued, raising her glass as the dishes rattled before her. "I want you to help me become a Shaper."

Her shaded eyes, as vacant as a statue's, sought him again.

"Yours is a completely unique situation," he commented. "There has never been a congenitally blind neuroparticipant—for obvious reasons. I'd have to consider all the aspects of the situation before I could advise you. Let's eat now, though. I'm starved."

"All right. But my blindness does not mean that I have never seen."

He did not ask her what she meant by that, because prime ribs were standing in front of him now and there

was a bottle of Chambertin at his elbow. He did pause
long enough to notice, though, as she raised her left
hand from beneath the table, that she wore no rings.

"I wonder if it's still snowing," he commented as they
drank their coffee. "It was coming down pretty hard
when I pulled into the dome."

"I hope so," she said, "even though it diffuses the
light and I can't 'see' anything at all through it. I like to
feel it falling about me and blowing against my face."

"How do you get about?"

"My dog, Sigmund—I gave him the night off," she
smiled, "—he can guide me anywhere. He's a mutie
Shepherd."

"Oh?" Render grew curious. "Can he talk much?"

She nodded.

"That operation wasn't as successful on him as on
some of them, though. He has a vocabulary of about
four hundred words, but I think it causes him pain to
speak. He's quite intelligent. You'll have to meet him
sometime."

Render began speculating immediately. He had spoken with such animals at recent medical conferences,
and had been startled by their combination of reasoning
ability and their devotion to their handlers. Much chro-
mosome tinkering, followed by delicate embryo-
surgery, was required to give a dog a brain capacity
greater than a chimpanzee's. Several followup operations were necessary to produce vocal abilities. Most
such experiments ended in failure, and the dozen or so
puppies a year on which they succeeded were valued in
the neighborhood of a hundred thousand dollars each.
He realized then, as he lit a cigarette and held the light
for a moment, that the stone in Miss Shallot's medallion
was a genuine ruby. He began to suspect that her
admission to a medical school might, in addition to her
academic record, have been based upon a sizeable
endowment to the college of her choice. Perhaps he was
being unfair though, he chided himself.

"Yes," he said, "we might do a paper on canine neuroses. Does he ever refer to his father as 'that son of a female Shepherd'?"

"He never met his father," she said, quite soberly. "He was raised apart from other dogs. His attitude could hardly be typical. I don't think you'll ever learn the functional psychology of the dog from a mutie."

"I imagine you're right," he dismissed it. "More coffee?"

"No, thanks."

Deciding it was time to continue the discussion, he said, "So you want to be a Shaper. . . ."

"Yes."

"I hate to be the one to destroy anybody's high ambitions," he told her. "Like poison, I hate it. Unless they have no foundation at all in reality. Then I can be ruthless. So—honestly, frankly, and in all sincerity, I do not see how it could ever be managed. Perhaps you're a fine psychiatrist—but in my opinion, it is a physical and mental impossibility for you ever to become a neuroparticipant. As for my reasons—"

"Wait," she said. "Not here, please. Humor me. I'm tired of this stuffy place—take me somewhere else to talk. I think I might be able to convince you there *is* a way."

"Why not?" he shrugged. "I have plenty of time. Sure—you call it. Where?"

"Blindspin?"

He suppressed an unwilling chuckle at the expression, but she laughed aloud.

"Fine," he said, "but I'm still thirsty."

A bottle of champagne was tallied and he signed the check despite her protests. It arrived in a colorful "Drink While You Drive" basket, and they stood then, and she was tall, but he was taller.

Blindspin.

A single name of a multitude of practices centered about the auto-driven auto. Flashing across the country

in the sure hands of an invisible chauffeur, windows all
opaque, night dark, sky high, tires assailing the road
below like four phantom buzzsaws—and starting from
scratch and ending in the same place, and never knowing where you are going or where you have been—it is
possible, for a moment, to kindle some feeling of
individuality in the coldest brainpan, to produce a
momentary awareness of self by virtue of an apartness
from all but a sense of motion. This is because movement through darkness is the ultimate abstraction of life
itself—at least that's what one of the Vital Comedians
said, and everybody in the place laughed.

Actually now, the phenomenon known as blindspin
first became prevalent (as might be suspected) among
certain younger members of the community, when
monitored highways deprived them of the means to
exercise their automobiles in some of the more individ-
ualistic ways which had come to be frowned upon by
the National Traffic Control Authority. Something had
to be done.

It was.

The first, disastrous reaction involved the simple
engineering feat of disconnecting the broadcast control
unit after one had entered onto a monitored highway. This resulted in the car's vanishing from the ken of
the monitor and passing back into the control of its occupants. Jealous as a deity, a monitor will not tolerate
that which denies its programmed omniscience: it will
thunder and lightning in the Highway Control Station nearest the point of last contact, sending winged
seraphs in search of that which has slipped from
sight.

Often, however, this was too late in happening, for the
roads are many and well-paved. Escape from detection
was, at first, relatively easy to achieve.

Other vehicles, though, necessarily behave as if a
rebel has no actual existence. Its presence cannot be
allowed for.

Boxed-in, on a heavily-traveled section of roadway,

the offender is subject to immediate annihilation in the event of any overall speedup or shift in traffic pattern which involves movement through his theoretically vacant position. This, in the early days of monitor-controls, caused a rapid series of collisions. Monitoring devices later became far more sophisticated, and mechanized cutoffs reduced the collision incidence subsequent to such an action. The quality of the pulpefactions and contusions which did occur, however, remained unaltered.

The next reaction was based on a thing which had been overlooked because it was obvious. The monitors took people where they wanted to go only because people told them they wanted to go there. A person pressing a random series of coordinates, without reference to any map, would either be left with a stalled automobile and a "RECHECK YOUR COORDINATES" light, or would suddenly be whisked away in any direction. The latter possesses a certain romantic appeal in that it offers speed, unexpected sights, and free hands. Also, it is perfectly legal; and it is possible to navigate all over two continents in this manner, if one is possessed of sufficient wherewithal and gluteal stamina.

As is the case in all such matters, the practice diffused upwards through the age brackets. Schoolteachers who only drove on Sundays fell into disrepute as selling points for used autos. Such is the way a world ends, said the entertainer.

End or no, the car designed to move on monitored highways is a mobile efficiency unit, complete with latrine, cupboard, refrigerator compartment, and gaming table. It also sleeps two with ease and four with some crowding. On occasion, three can be a real crowd.

Render drove out of the dome and into the marginal aisle. He halted the car.

"Want to jab some coordinates?" he asked.

"You do it. My fingers know too many."

Render punched random buttons. The Spinner

moved onto the highway. Render asked speed of the vehicle then, and it moved into the high-acceleration lane.

The Spinner's lights burnt holes in the darkness. The city backed away fast; it was a smouldering bonfire on both sides of the road, stirred by sudden gusts of wind, hidden by white swirlings, obscured by the steady fall of gray ash. Render knew his speed was only about sixty percent of what it would have been on a clear, dry night.

He did not blank the windows, but leaned back and stared out through them. Eileen "looked" ahead into what light there was. Neither of them said anything for ten or fifteen minutes.

The city shrank to sub-city as they sped on. After a time, short sections of open road began to appear.

"Tell me what it looks like outside," she said.

"Why didn't you ask me to describe your dinner, or the suit of armor beside our table?"

"Because I tasted one and felt the other. This is different."

"There is snow falling outside. Take it away and what you have left is black."

"What else?"

"There is slush on the road. When it starts to freeze, traffic will drop to a crawl unless we outrun this storm. The slush looks like an old, dark syrup, just starting to get sugary on top."

"Anything else?"

"That's it, lady."

"Is it snowing harder or less hard than when we left the club?"

"Harder, I should say."

"Would you pour me a drink?" she asked him.

"Certainly."

They turned their seats inward and Render raised the table. He fetched two glasses from the cupboard.

"Your health," said Render, after he had poured.

"Here's looking at you."

Render downed his drink. She sipped hers. He waited

for her next comment. He knew that two cannot play at the Socratic game, and he expected more questions before she said what she wanted to say.

She said: "What is the most beautiful thing you have ever seen?"

Yes, he decided, he had guessed correctly.

He replied without hesitation: "The sinking of Atlantis."

"I was serious."

"So was I."

"Would you care to elaborate?"

"I sank Atlantis," he said, "personally.

"It was about three years ago. And God! it was lovely! It was all ivory towers and golden minarets and silver balconies. There were bridges of opal, and crimson pennants and a milk-white river flowing between lemon-colored banks. There were jade steeples, and trees as old as the world tickling the bellies of clouds, and ships in the great sea-harbor of Xanadu, as delicately constructed as musical instruments, all swaying with the tides. The twelve princes of the realm held court in the dozen-pillared Coliseum of the Zodiac, to listen to a Greek tenor sax play at sunset.

"The Greek, of course, was a patient of mine— paranoiac. The etiology of the thing is rather complicated, but that's what I wandered into inside his mind. I gave him free rein for awhile, and in the end I had to split Atlantis in half and sink it full fathom five. He's playing again and you've doubtless heard his sounds, if you like such sounds at all. He's good. I still see him periodically, but he is no longer the last descendant of the greatest minstrel of Atlantis. He's just a fine, late twentieth-century saxman.

"Sometimes though, as I look back on the apocalypse I worked within his vision of grandeur, I experience a fleeting sense of lost beauty—because, for a single moment, his abnormally intense feelings were my feelings, and he felt that his dream was the most beautiful thing in the world."

He refilled their glasses.

"That wasn't exactly what I meant," she said.

"I know."

"I meant something real."

"It was more real than real, I assure you."

"I don't doubt it, but . . ."

"—But I destroyed the foundation you were laying for your argument. Okay, I apologize. I'll hand it back to you. Here's something that could be real:

"We are moving along the edge of a great bowl of sand," he said. "Into it, the snow is gently drifting. In the spring the snow will melt, the waters will run down into the earth, or be evaporated away by the heat of the sun. Then only the sand will remain. Nothing grows in the sand, except for an occasional cactus. Nothing lives here but snakes, a few birds, insects, burrowing things, and a wandering coyote or two. In the afternoon these things will look for shade. Any place where there's an old fence post or a rock or a skull or a cactus to block out the sun, there you will witness life cowering before the elements. But the colors are beyond belief, and the elements are more lovely, almost, than the things they destroy."

"There is no such place near here," she said.

"If I say it, then there is. Isn't there? I've seen it."

"Yes . . . You're right."

"And it doesn't matter if it's a painting by a woman named O'Keeffe, or something right outside our window, does it? If I've seen it?"

"I acknowledge the truth of the diagnosis," she said. "Do you want to speak it for me?"

"No, go ahead."

He refilled the small glasses once more.

"The damage is in my eyes," she told him, "not my brain."

He lit her cigarette.

"I can see with other eyes if I can enter other brains."

He lit his own cigarette.

"Neuroparticipation is based upon the fact that two

nervous systems can share the same impulses, the same fantasies. . . ."

"*Controlled* fantasies."

"I could perform therapy and at the same time experience genuine visual impressions."

"No," said Render.

"You don't know what it's like to be cut off from a whole area of stimuli! To know that a Mongoloid idiot can experience something you can never know—and that he cannot appreciate it because, like you, he was condemned before birth in a court of biological happenstance, in a place where there is no justice—only fortuity, pure and simple."

"The universe did not invent justice. Man did. Unfortunately, man must reside in the universe."

"I'm not asking the universe to help me—I'm asking you."

"I'm sorry," said Render.

"Why won't you help me?"

"At this moment you are demonstrating my main reason."

"Which is . . . ?"

"Emotion. This thing means far too much to you. When the therapist is in-phase with a patient he is narco-electrically removed from most of his own bodily sensations. This is necessary—because his mind must be completely absorbed by the task at hand. It is also necessary that his emotions undergo a similar suspension. This, of course, is impossible in the one sense that a person always emotes to some degree. But the therapist's emotions are sublimated into a generalized feeling of exhilaration—or, as in my own case, into an artistic reverie. With you, however, the 'seeing' would be too much. You would be in constant danger of losing control of the dream."

"I disagree with you."

"Of course you do. But the fact remains that you would be dealing, and dealing constantly, with the abnormal. The power of a neurosis is unimaginable to

ninety-nine point etcetera percent of the population,
because we can never adequately judge the intensity of
our own—let alone those of others, when we only see
them from the outside. That is why no neuroparticipant
will ever undertake to treat a full-blown psychotic. The
few pioneers in that area are all themselves in therapy
today. It would be like diving into a maelstrom. If the
therapist loses the upper hand in an intense session he
becomes the Shaped rather than the Shaper. The syn-
apses respond like a fission reaction when nervous
impulses are artificially augmented. The transference
effect is almost instantaneous.

"I did an awful lot of skiing five years ago. This is
because I was a claustrophobe. I had to run and it took
me six months to beat the thing—all because of one tiny
lapse that occurred in a measureless fraction of an
instant. I had to refer the patient to another therapist.
And this was only a minor repercussion.—If you were
to go ga-ga over the scenery, girl, you could wind up in a
rest home for life."

She finished her drink and Render refilled the glass.
The night raced by. They had left the city far behind
them, and the road was open and clear. The darkness
eased more and more of itself between the falling flakes.
The Spinner picked up speed.

"All right," she admitted, "maybe you're right. Still,
though, I think you can help me."

"How?" he asked.

"Accustom me to seeing, so that the images will lose
their novelty, the emotions wear off. Accept me as a
patient and rid me of my sight-anxiety. Then what you
have said so far will cease to apply. I will be able to
undertake the training then, and give my full attention
to therapy. I'll be able to sublimate the sight-pleasure
into something else."

Render wondered.

Perhaps it could be done. It would be a difficult
undertaking, though.

It might also make therapeutic history.

No one was really qualified to try it, because no one had ever tried it before.

But Eileen Shallot was a rarity—no, a unique item—for it was likely she was the only person in the world who combined the necessary technical background with the unique problem.

He drained his glass, refilled it, refilled hers.

He was still considering the problem as the "RE-COORDINATE" light came on and the car pulled into a cutoff and stood there. He switched off the buzzer and sat there for a long while, thinking.

It was not often that other persons heard him acknowledge his feelings regarding his skill. His colleagues considered him modest. Offhand, though, it might be noted that he was aware that the day a better neuroparticipant began practicing would be the day that a troubled homo sapiens was to be treated by something but immeasurably less than angels.

Two drinks remained. Then he tossed the emptied bottle into the backbin.

"You know something?" he finally said.

"What?"

"It might be worth a try."

He swiveled about then and leaned forward to recoordinate, but she was there first. As he pressed the buttons and the S-7 swung around, she kissed him. Below her dark glasses her cheeks were moist.

II

The suicide bothered him more than it should have, and Mrs. Lambert had called the day before to cancel her appointment. So Render decided to spend the morning being pensive. Accordingly, he entered the office wearing a cigar and a frown.

"Did you see . . . ?" asked Mrs. Hedges.

"Yes." He pitched his coat onto the table that stood in the far corner of the room. He crossed to the window, stared down. "Yes," he repeated, "I was driving by with my windows clear. They were still cleaning up when I passed."

"Did you know him?"

"I don't even know the name yet. How could I?"

"Priss Tully just called me—she's a receptionist for that engineering outfit up on the eighty-sixth. She says it was James Irizarry, an ad designer who had offices down the hall from them.—That's a long way to fall. He must have been unconscious when he hit, huh? He bounced off the building. If you open the window and lean out you can see—off to the left there —where . . ."

"Never mind, Bennie. —Your friend have any idea why he did it?"

"Not really. His secretary came running up the hall, screaming. Seems she went in his office to see him about some drawings, just as he was getting up over the sill. There was a note on his board. 'I've had everything I wanted,' it said. 'Why wait around?' Sort of funny, huh? I don't mean *funny*. . . ."

"Yeah.—Know anything about his personal affairs?"

"Married. Coupla kids. Good professional rep. Lots of business. Sober as anybody.—He could afford an office in this building."

"Good Lord!" Render turned. "Have you got a case file there or something?"

"You know," she shrugged her thick shoulders, "I've got friends all over this hive. We always talk when things go slow. Prissy's my sister-in-law, anyhow—"

"You mean that if I dived through this window right now, my current biography would make the rounds in the next five minutes?"

"Probably," she twisted her bright lips into a smile, "give or take a couple. But don't do it today, huh?—You know, it would be kind of anticlimactic, and it wouldn't get the same coverage as a solus.

"Anyhow," she continued, "you're a mind-mixer. You wouldn't do it."

"You're betting against statistics," he observed. "The medical profession, along with attorneys, manages about three times as many as most other work areas."

"Hey!" She looked worried. "Go 'way from my window!

"I'd have to go to work for Doctor Hanson then," she added, "and he's a slob."

He moved to her desk.

"I never know when to take you seriously," she decided.

"I appreciate your concern," he nodded, "indeed I do. As a matter of fact, I have never been statistic-prone—I should have repercussed out of the neuropy game four years ago."

"You'd be a headline, though," she mused. "All those reporters asking me about you . . . Hey, why do they do it, huh?"

"Who?"

"Anybody."

"How should I know, Bennie? I'm only a humble psyche-stirrer. If I could pinpoint a general underlying cause—and then maybe figure a way to anticipate the thing—why, it might even be better than my jumping, for newscopy. But I can't do it, because there is no single, simple reason—I don't think."

"Oh."

"About thirty-five years ago it was the ninth leading cause of death in the United States. Now it's number six for North and South America. I think it's seventh in Europe."

"And nobody will ever really know why Irizarry jumped?"

Render swung a chair backward and seated himself. He knocked an ash into her petite and gleaming tray. She emptied it into the waste-chute, hastily, and coughed a significant cough.

"Oh, one can always speculate," he said, "and one in my profession will. The first thing to consider would be the personality traits which might predispose a man to periods of depression. People who keep their emotions under rigid control, people who are conscientious and rather compulsively concerned with small matters . . ." He knocked another fleck of ash into her tray and watched as she reached out to dump it, then quickly drew her hand back again. He grinned an evil grin. "In short," he finished, "some of the characteristics of people in professions which require individual, rather than group performance—medicine, law, the arts."

She regarded him speculatively.

"Don't worry though," he chuckled, "I'm pleased as hell with life."

"You're kind of down in the mouth this morning."

"Pete called me. He broke his ankle yesterday in gym class. They ought to supervise those things more closely. I'm thinking of changing his school."

"Again?"

"Maybe. I'll see. The headmaster is going to call me this afternoon. I don't like to keep shuffling him, but I do want him to finish school in one piece."

"A kid can't grow up without an accident or two. It's—statistics."

"Statistics aren't the same thing as destiny, Bennie. Everybody makes his own."

"Statistics or destiny?"

"Both, I guess."

"I think that if something's going to happen, it's going to happen."

"I don't. I happen to think that the human will, backed by a sane mind, can exercise some measure of control over events. If I didn't think so, I wouldn't be in the racket I'm in."

"The world's a machine—you know—cause, effect. Statistics do imply the prob—"

"The human mind is not a machine, and I do not know cause and effect. Nobody does."

"You have a degree in chemistry, as I recall. You're a scientist, Doc."

"So I'm a Trotskyite deviationist," he smiled, stretching, "and you were once a ballet teacher." He got to his feet and picked up his coat.

"By the way, Miss DeVille called, left a message. She said: 'How about St. Moritz?' "

"Too ritzy," he decided aloud. "It's going to be Davos."

Because the suicide bothered him more than it should have, Render closed the door to his office and turned off the windows and turned on the phonograph. He put on the desk light only.

How has the quality of human life been changed, he wrote, *since the beginnings of the industrial revolution?*

He picked up the paper and reread the sentence. It was the topic he had been asked to discuss that coming Saturday. As was typical in such cases he did not know what to say because he had too much to say, and only an hour to say it in.

He got up and began to pace the office, now filled with Beethoven's Eighth Symphony.

"The power to hurt," he said, snapping on a lapel microphone and activating his recorder, "has evolved in a direct relationship to technological advancement." His imaginary audience grew quiet. He smiled. "Man's potential for working simple mayhem has been multiplied by mass-production; his capacity for injuring the psyche through personal contacts has expanded in an exact ratio to improved communication facilities. But these are all matters of common knowledge, and are not the things I wish to consider tonight. Rather, I should like to discuss what I choose to call autopsychomimesis —the self-generated anxiety complexes which on first scrutiny appear quite similar to classic patterns, but which actually represent radical dispersions of psychic energy. They are peculiar to our times. . . ."

He paused to dispose of his cigar and formulate his next words.

"Autopsychomimesis," he thought aloud, "a self-perpetuated imitation complex—almost an attention-getting affair.—A jazzman, for example, who acted hopped-up half the time, even though he had never used an addictive narcotic and only dimly remembered anyone who had—because all the stimulants and tranquilizers of today are quite benign. Like Quixote, he aspired after a legend when his music alone should have been sufficient outlet for his tensions.

"Or my Korean War Orphan, alive today by virtue of the Red Cross and UNICEF and foster parents whom he never met. He wanted a family so badly that he made one up. And what then?—He hated his imaginary father and he loved his imaginary mother quite dearly—for he was a highly intelligent boy, and he too longed after the half-true complexes of tradition. Why?

"Today, everyone is sophisticated enough to understand the time-honored patterns of psychic disturbance. Today, many of the reasons for those disturbances have been removed—not as radically as my now-adult war orphan's, but with as remarkable an effect. We are living in a neurotic past.—Again, why? Because our present times are geared to physical health, security, and well-being. We have abolished hunger, though the backwoods orphan would still rather receive a package of food concentrates from a human being who cares for him than to obtain a warm meal from an automat unit in the middle of the jungle.

"Physical welfare is now every man's right, in excess. The reaction to this has occurred in the area of mental health. Thanks to technology, the reasons for many of the old social problems have passed, and along with them went many of the reasons for psychic distress. But between the black of yesterday and the white of tomorrow is the great gray of today, filled with nostalgia and fear of the future, which cannot be expressed on a purely material plane, is now being represented by a willful seeking after historical anxiety-modes. . . ."

The phone-box buzzed briefly. Render did not hear it over the Eighth.

"We are afraid of what we do not know," he continued, "and tomorrow is a very great unknown. My own specialized area of psychiatry did not even exist thirty years ago. Science is capable of advancing itself so rapidly now that there is a genuine public uneasiness—I might even say 'distress'—as to the logical outcome: the total mechanization of everything in the world. . . ."

He passed near the desk as the phone buzzed again. He switched off his microphone and softened the Eighth.

"Hello?"

"St. Moritz," she said.

"Davos," he replied firmly.

"Charlie, you are most exasperating!"

"Jill, dear—so are you."

"Shall we discuss it tonight?"

"There is nothing to discuss!"

"You'll pick me up at five, though?"

He hesitated, then:

"Yes, at five. How come the screen is blank?"

"I've had my hair fixed. I'm going to surprise you again."

He suppressed an idiot chuckle, said, "Pleasantly, I hope. Okay, see you then," waited for her "goodbye," and broke the connection.

He transpared the windows, turned off the light on his desk, and looked outside.

Gray again overhead, and many slow flakes of snow—wandering, not being blown about much—moving downward and then losing themselves in the tumult. . . .

He also saw, when he opened the window and leaned out, the place off to the left where Irizarry had left his next-to-last mark on the world.

He closed the window and listened to the rest of the symphony. It had been a week since he had gone blindspinning with Eileen. Her appointment was for one o'clock.

He remembered her fingertips brushing over his face, like leaves, or the bodies of insects, learning his appearance in the ancient manner of the blind. The memory was not altogether pleasant. He wondered why.

Far below, a patch of hosed pavement was blank once again; under a thin, fresh shroud of white, it was slippery as glass. A building custodian hurried outside and spread salt on it, before someone slipped and hurt himself.

Sigmund was the myth of Fenris come alive. After Render had instructed Mrs. Hedges, "Show them in," the door had begun to open, was suddenly pushed wider, and a pair of smoky-yellow eyes stared in at him. The eyes were set in a strangely misshapen dog-skull.

Sigmund's was not a low canine brow, slanting up slightly from the muzzle; it was a high, shaggy cranium, making the eyes appear even more deep-set than they actually were. Render shivered slightly at the size and

aspect of that head. The muties he had seen had all been
puppies. Sigmund was full grown, and his gray-black fur
had a tendency to bristle, which made him appear
somewhat larger than a normal specimen of the breed.

He stared in at Render in a very un-doglike way and
made a growling noise which sounded too much like,
"Hello, doctor," to have been an accident.

Render nodded and stood.

"Hello, Sigmund," he said. "Come in."

The dog turned his head, sniffing the air of the
room—as though deciding whether or not to trust his
ward within its confines. Then he returned his stare to
Render, dipped his head in an affirmative, and shoul-
dered the door open. Perhaps the entire encounter had
taken only one disconcerting second.

Eileen followed him, holding lightly to the double-
leashed harness. The dog padded soundlessly across the
thick rug—head low, as though he was stalking something. His eyes never left Render's.

"So this is Sigmund . . . ? How are you, Eileen?"

"Fine.—Yes, he wanted very badly to come along,
and I wanted you to meet him."

Render led her to a chair and seated her. She
unsnapped the double guide from the dog's harness and
placed it on the floor. Sigmund sat down beside it and
continued to stare at Render.

"How is everything at State Psych?"

"Same as always.—May I bum a cigarette, doctor? I
forgot mine."

He placed it between her fingers, furnished a light.
She was wearing a dark blue suit and her glasses were
flame blue. The silver spot on her forehead reflected the
glow of his lighter; she continued to stare at that point in
space after he had withdrawn his hand. Her shoulder-
length hair appeared a trifle lighter than it had seemed
on the night they met; today it was like a fresh-minted
copper coin.

Render seated himself on the corner of his desk,
drawing up his world-ashtray with his toe.

"You told me before that being blind did not mean

that you had never seen. I didn't ask you to explain it
then. But I'd like to ask you now."

"I had a neuroparticipation session with Doctor
Riscomb," she told him, "before he had his accident.
He wanted to accommodate my mind to visual impressions. Unfortunately, there was never a second session."

"I see. What did you do in that session?"

She crossed her ankles and Render noted they were
well-turned.

"Colors, mostly. The experience was quite overwhelming."

"How well do you remember them? How long ago
was it?"

"About six months ago—and I shall never forget
them. I have even dreamt in color patterns since then."

"How often?"

"Several times a week."

"What sort of associations do they carry?"

"Nothing special. They just come into my mind along
with other stimuli now—in a pretty haphazard way."

"How?"

"Well, for instance, when you ask me a question it's a
sort of yellowish-orangish pattern that I 'see.' Your
greeting was a kind of silvery thing. Now that you're just
sitting there listening to me, saying nothing, I associate
you with a deep, almost violet, blue."

Sigmund shifted his gaze to the desk and stared at the
side panel.

Can he hear the recorder spinning inside? wondered
Render. *And if he can, can he guess what it is and what it's
doing?*

If so, the dog would doubtless tell Eileen—not that
she was unaware of what was now an accepted practice
—and she might not like being reminded that he
considered her case as therapy, rather than a mere
mechanical adaptation process. If he thought it would
do any good (he smiled inwardly at the notion), he
would talk to the dog in private about it.

Inwardly, he shrugged.

"I'll construct a rather elementary fantasy world then," he said finally, "and introduce you to some basic forms today."

She smiled; and Render looked down at the myth who crouched by her side, its tongue a piece of beefsteak hanging over a picket fence.

Is he smiling too?

"Thank you," she said.

Sigmund wagged his tail.

"Well then," Render disposed of his cigarette near Madagascar, "I'll fetch out the 'egg' now and test it. In the meantime," he pressed an unobtrusive button, "perhaps some music would prove relaxing."

She started to reply, but a Wagnerian overture snuffed out the words. Render jammed the button again, and there was a moment of silence during which he said, "Heh heh. Thought Respighi was next."

It took two more pushes for him to locate some Roman pines.

"You could have left him on," she observed. "I'm quite fond of Wagner."

"No thanks," he said, opening the closet, "I'd keep stepping in all those piles of leitmotifs."

The great egg drifted out into the office, soundless as a cloud. Render heard a soft growl behind as he drew it toward the desk. He turned quickly.

Like the shadow of a bird, Sigmund had gotten to his feet, crossed the room, and was already circling the machine and sniffing at it—tail taut, ears flat, teeth bared.

"Easy, Sig," said Render. "It's an Omnichannel Neural T & R Unit. It won't bite or anything like that. It's just a machine, like a car, or a teevee, or a dishwasher. That's what we're going to use today to show Eileen what some things look like."

"Don't like it," rumbled the dog.

"Why?"

Sigmund had no reply, so he stalked back to Eileen and laid his head in her lap.

"Don't like it," he repeated, looking up at her.

"Why?"

"No words," he decided. "We go home now?"

"No," she answered him. "You're going to curl up in the corner and take a nap, and I'm going to curl up in that machine and do the same thing—sort of."

"No good," he said, tail drooping.

"Go on now," she pushed him, "lie down and behave yourself."

He acquiesced, but he whined when Render blanked the windows and touched the button which transformed his desk into the operator's seat.

He whined once more—when the egg, connected now to an outlet, broke in the middle and the top slid back and up, revealing the interior.

Render seated himself. His chair became a contour couch and moved in halfway beneath the console. He sat upright and it moved back again, becoming a chair. He touched a part of the desk and half the ceiling disengaged itself, reshaped itself, and lowered to hover overhead like a huge bell. He stood and moved around to the side of the ro-womb. Respighi spoke of pines and such, and Render disengaged an earphone from beneath the egg and leaned back across his desk. Blocking one ear with his shoulder and pressing the microphone to the other, he played upon the buttons with his free hand. Leagues of surf drowned the tone poem; miles of traffic overrode it; a great clanging bell sent fracture lines running through it; and the feedback said: ". . . Now that you are just sitting there listening to me, saying nothing, I associate you with a deep, almost violet, blue. . . ."

He switched to the face mask and monitored, *one*— cinnamon, *two*—leaf mold, *three*—deep reptilian musk . . . and down through thirst, and the tastes of honey and vinegar and salt, and back on up through lilacs and wet concrete, a before-the-storm whiff of ozone, and all the basic olfactory and gustatory cues for morning, afternoon, and evening in the town.

The couch floated normally in its pool of mercury, magnetically stabilized by the walls of the egg. He set the tapes.

The ro-womb was in perfect condition.

"Okay," said Render, turning, "everything checks."

She was just placing her glasses atop her folded garments. She had undressed while Render was testing the machine. He was perturbed by her narrow waist, her large, dark-pointed breasts, her long legs. She was too well-formed for a woman her height, he decided.

He realized though, as he stared at her, that his main annoyance was, of course, the fact that she was his patient.

"Ready here," she said, and he moved to her side.

He took her elbow and guided her to the machine. Her fingers explored its interior. As he helped her enter the unit, he saw that her eyes were a vivid sea-green. Of this, too, he disapproved.

"Comfortable?"

"Yes."

"Okay then, we're set. I'm going to close it now. Sweet dreams."

The upper shell dropped slowly. Closed, it grew opaque, then dazzling. Render was staring down at his own distorted reflection.

He moved back in the direction of his desk.

Sigmund was on his feet, blocking the way.

Render reached down to pat his head, but the dog jerked it aside.

"Take me, with," he growled.

"I'm afraid that can't be done, old fellow," said Render. "Besides, we're not really going anywhere. We'll just be dozing right here, in this room."

The dog did not seem mollified.

"Why?"

Render sighed. An argument with a dog was about the most ludicrous thing he could imagine when sober.

"Sig," he said, "I'm trying to help her learn what things look like. You doubtless do a fine job guiding her around in this world which she cannot see—but she needs to know what it looks like now, and I'm going to show her."

"Then she, will not, need me."

"Of course she will." Render almost laughed. The pathetic thing was here bound so closely to the absurd thing that he could not help it. "I can't restore her sight," he explained. "I'm just going to transfer her some sight-abstractions—sort of lend her my eyes for a short time. Savvy?"

"No," said the dog. "Take mine."

Render turned off the music.

The whole mutie-master relationship might be worth six volumes, he decided, *in German*.

He pointed to the far corner.

"Lie down, over there, like Eileen told you. This isn't going to take long, and when it's all over you're going to leave the same way you came—you leading. Okay?"

Sigmund did not answer, but he turned and moved off to the corner, tail drooping again.

Render seated himself and lowered the hood, the operator's modified version of the ro-womb. He was alone before the ninety white buttons and the two red ones. The world ended in the blackness beyond the console. He loosened his necktie and unbuttoned his collar.

He removed the helmet from its receptacle and checked its leads. Donning it then, he swung the halfmask up over his lower face and dropped the darksheet down to meet with it. He rested his right arm in the sling, and with a single tapping gesture, he eliminated his patient's consciousness.

A Shaper does not press white buttons consciously. He wills conditions. Then deeply-implanted muscular reflexes exert an almost imperceptible pressure against the sensitive arm-sling, which glides into the proper position and encourages an extended finger to move forward. A button is pressed. The sling moves on.

Render felt a tingling at the base of his skull; he smelled fresh-cut grass.

Suddenly he was moving up the great gray alley between the worlds.

After what seemed a long time, Render felt that he was footed on a strange Earth. He could see nothing; it was only a sense of presence that informed him he had arrived. It was the darkest of all the dark nights he had ever known.

He willed that the darkness disperse. Nothing happened.

A part of his mind came awake again, a part he had not realized was sleeping; he recalled whose world he had entered.

He listened for her presence. He heard fear and anticipation.

He willed color. First, red . . .

He felt a correspondence. Then there was an echo.

Everything became red; he inhabited the center of an infinite ruby.

Orange. Yellow . . .

He was caught in a piece of amber.

Green now, and he added the exhalations of a sultry sea. Blue, and the coolness of evening.

He stretched his mind then, producing all the colors at once. They came in great swirling plumes.

Then he tore them apart and forced a form upon them.

An incandescent rainbow arched across the black sky.

He fought for browns and grays below him. Self-luminescent, they appeared—in shimmering, shifting patches.

Somewhere, a sense of awe. There was no trace of hysteria though, so he continued with the Shaping.

He managed a horizon, and the blackness drained

away beyond it. The sky grew faintly blue, and he
ventured a herd of dark clouds. There was resistance to
his efforts at creating distance and depth, so he rein-
forced the tableau with a very faint sound of surf. A
transference from an auditory concept of distance came
on slowly then, as he pushed the clouds about. Quickly,
he threw up a high forest to offset a rising wave of
acrophobia.

The panic vanished.

Render focused his attention on tall trees—oaks and
pines, poplars and sycamores. He hurled them about
like spears, in ragged arrays of greens and browns and
yellows, unrolled a thick mat of morning-moist grass,
dropped a series of gray boulders and greenish logs at
irregular intervals, and tangled and twined the
branches overhead, casting a uniform shade throughout
the glen.

The effect was staggering. It seemed as if the entire
world was shaken with a sob, then silent.

Through the stillness he felt her presence. He had
decided it would be best to lay the groundwork quickly,
to set up a tangible headquarters, to prepare a field for
operations. He could backtrack later, he could repair
and amend the results of the trauma in the sessions yet
to come; but this much, at least, was necessary for a
beginning.

With a start, he realized that the silence was not a
withdrawal. Eileen had made herself immanent in the
trees and the grass, the stones and the bushes; she was
personalizing their forms, relating them to tactile sensations, sounds, temperatures, aromas.

With a soft breeze, he stirred the branches of the
trees. Just beyond the bounds of seeing he worked out
the splashing sounds of a brook.

There was a feeling of joy. He shared it.

She was bearing it extremely well, so he decided to
extend the scope of the exercise. He let his mind wander
among the trees, experiencing a momentary doubl-

ing of vision, during which time he saw an enormous hand riding in an aluminum carriage toward a circle of white.

He was beside the brook now and he was seeking her, carefully.

He drifted with the water. He had not yet taken on a form. The splashes became a gurgling as he pushed the brook through shallow places and over rocks. At his insistence, the waters became more articulate.

"Where are you?" asked the brook.

Here! Here!

Here!

. . . and here! replied the trees, the bushes, the stones, the grass.

"Choose one," said the brook, as it widened, rounded a mass of rock, then bent its way toward a slope, heading toward a blue pool.

I cannot, was the answer from the wind.

"You must." The brook widened and poured itself into the pool, swirled about the surface, then stilled itself and reflected branches and dark clouds. "Now!"

Very well, echoed the wood, *in a moment.*

The mist rose above the lake and drifted to the bank of the pool.

"Now," tinkled the mist.

Here, then . . .

She had chosen a small willow. It swayed in the wind; it trailed its branches in the water.

"Eileen Shallot," he said, "regard the lake."

The breezes shifted; the willow bent.

It was not difficult for him to recall her face, her body. The tree spun as though rootless. Eileen stood in the midst of a quiet explosion of leaves; she stared, frightened, into the deep blue mirror of Render's mind, the lake.

She covered her face with her hands, but it could not stop the seeing.

"Behold yourself," said Render.

She lowered her hands and peered downwards. Then she turned in every direction, slowly; she studied herself. Finally:

"I feel I am quite lovely," she said. "Do I feel so because you want me to, or is it true?"

She looked all about as she spoke, seeking the Shaper.

"It is true," said Render, from everywhere.

"Thank you."

There was a swirl of white and she was wearing a belted garment of damask. The light in the distance brightened almost imperceptibly. A faint touch of pink began at the base of the lowest cloudbank.

"What is happening there?" she asked, facing that direction.

"I am going to show you a sunrise," said Render, "and I shall probably botch it a bit—but then, it's my first professional sunrise under these circumstances."

"Where are *you*?" she asked.

"Everywhere," he replied.

"Please take on a form so that I can see you."

"All right."

"Your natural form."

He willed that he be beside her on the bank, and he was.

Startled by a metallic flash, he looked downward. The world receded for an instant, then grew stable once again. He laughed, and the laugh froze as he thought of something.

He was wearing the suit of armor which had stood beside their table in The Partridge and Scalpel on the night they met.

She reached out and touched it.

"The suit of armor by our table," she acknowledged, running her fingertips over the plates and the junctures. "I associated it with you that night."

". . . And you stuffed me into it just now," he commented. "You're a strong-willed woman."

The armor vanished and he was wearing his

graybrown suit and looseknit bloodclot necktie and a professional expression.

"Behold the real me," he smiled faintly. "Now, to the sunset. I'm going to use all the colors. Watch!"

They seated themselves on the green park bench which had appeared behind them, and Render pointed in the direction he had decided upon as east.

Slowly, the sun worked through its morning attitudes. For the first time in this particular world it shone down like a god, and reflected off the lake, and broke the clouds, and set the landscape to smouldering beneath the mist that arose from the moist wood.

Watching, watching intently, staring directly into the ascending bonfire, Eileen did not move for a long while, nor speak. Render could sense her fascination.

She was staring at the source of all light; it reflected back from the gleaming coin on her brow, like a single drop of blood.

Render said, "That is the sun, and those are clouds," and he clapped his hands and the clouds covered the sun and there was a soft rumble overhead, "and that is thunder," he finished.

The rain fell then, shattering the lake and tickling their faces, making sharp striking sounds on the leaves, then soft tapping sounds, dripping down from the branches overhead, soaking their garments and plastering their hair, running down their necks and falling into their eyes, turning patches of brown earth to mud.

A splash of lightning covered the sky, and a second later there was another peal of thunder.

". . . And this is a summer storm," he lectured. "You see how the rain affects the foliage, and ourselves. What you just saw in the sky before the thunderclap was lightning."

". . . Too much," she said. "Let up on it for a moment, please."

The rain stopped instantly and the sun broke through the clouds.

"I have the damnedest desire for a cigarette," she said, "but I left mine in another world."

As she said it one appeared, already lighted, between her fingers.

"It's going to taste rather flat," said Render strangely. He watched her for a moment, then:

"I didn't give you that cigarette," he noted. "You picked it from my mind."

The smoke laddered and spiraled upward, was swept away.

". . . Which means that, for the second time today, I have underestimated the pull of that vacuum in your mind—in the place where sight ought to be. You are assimilating these new impressions very rapidly. You're even going to the extent of groping after new ones. Be careful. Try to contain that impulse."

"It's like a hunger," she said.

"Perhaps we had best conclude this session now."

Their clothing was dry again. A bird began to sing.

"No, wait! Please! I'll be careful. I want to see more things."

"There is always the next visit," said Render. "But I suppose we can manage one more. Is there something you want very badly to see?"

"Yes. Winter. Snow."

"Okay," smiled the Shaper, "then wrap yourself in that furpiece. . . ."

The afternoon slipped by rapidly after the departure of his patient. Render was in a good mood. He felt emptied and filled again. He had come through the first trial without suffering any repercussions. He decided that he was going to succeed. His satisfaction was greater than his fear. It was with a sense of exhilaration that he returned to working on his speech.

". . . And what is the power to hurt?" he inquired of the microphone.

"We live by pleasure and we live by pain," he answered himself. "Either can frustrate and either can encourage. But while pleasure and pain are rooted in biology, they are conditioned by society: thus are values to be derived. Because of the enormous masses of humanity, hectically changing positions in space every day throughout the cities of the world, there has come into necessary being a series of totally inhuman controls upon these movements. Every day they nibble their way into new areas—driving our cars, flying our planes, interviewing us, diagnosing our diseases—and I cannot even venture a moral judgment upon these intrusions. They have become necessary. Ultimately, they may prove salutary.

"The point I wish to make, however, is that we are often unaware of our own values. We cannot honestly tell what a thing means to us until it is removed from our life-situation. If an object of value ceases to exist, then the psychic energies which were bound up in it are released. We seek after new objects of value in which to invest this—mana, if you like, or libido, if you don't. And no one thing which has vanished during the past three or four or five decades was, in itself, massively significant; and no new thing which came into being during that time is massively malicious toward the people it has replaced or the people it in some manner controls. A society, though, is made up of many things, and when these things are changed too rapidly the results are unpredictable. An intense study of mental illness is often quite revealing as to the nature of the stresses in the society where the illness was made. If anxiety-patterns fall into special groups and classes, then something of the discontent of society can be learned from them. Carl Jung pointed out that when consciousness is repeatedly frustrated in a quest for values it will turn its search to the unconscious; failing there, it will proceed to quarry its way into the hypothetical collective unconscious. He noted, in the postwar analyses of ex-Nazis, that the longer they searched for something to erect from the ruins of their lives—having lived through a period of classical iconoclasm, and then

seen their new ideals topple as well—the longer they
searched, the further back they seemed to reach into
the collective unconscious of their people. Their
dreams themselves came to take on patterns out of the
Teutonic mythos.

"This, in a much less dramatic sense, is happening
today. There are historical periods when the group
tendency for the mind to turn in upon itself, to turn
back, is greater than at other times. We are living in
such a period of Quixotism, in the original sense of the
term. This is because the power to hurt, in our time, is
the power to ignore, to baffle—and it is no longer the
exclusive property of human beings—"

A buzz interrupted him then. He switched off the
recorder, touched the phone-box.

"Charles Render speaking," he told it.

"This is Paul Charter," lisped the box. "I am headmaster at Dilling."

"Yes?"

The picture cleared. Render saw a man whose eyes
were set close together beneath a high forehead. The
forehead was heavily creased; the mouth twitched as it
spoke.

"Well, I want to apologize again for what happened. It
was a faulty piece of equipment that caused—"

"Can't you afford proper facilities? Your fees are high
enough."

"It was a *new* piece of equipment. It was a factory
defect—"

"Wasn't there anybody in charge of the class?"

"Yes, but—"

"Why didn't he inspect the equipment? Why wasn't he
on hand to prevent the fall?"

"He *was* on hand, but it happened too fast for him to
do anything. As for inspecting the equipment for factory
defects, that isn't his job. Look, I'm very sorry. I'm quite
fond of your boy. I can assure you nothing like this will
ever happen again."

"You're right, there. But that's because I'm picking

him up tomorrow morning and enrolling him in a school that exercises proper safety precautions."

Render ended the conversation with a flick of his finger. After several minutes had passed he stood and crossed the room to his small wall safe, which was partly masked, though not concealed, by a shelf of books. It took only a moment for him to open it and withdraw a jewel box containing a cheap necklace and a framed photograph of a man resembling himself, though somewhat younger, and a woman whose up-swept hair was dark and whose chin was small, and two youngsters between them—the girl holding the baby in her arms and forcing her bright bored smile on ahead. Render always stared for only a few seconds on such occasions, fondling the necklace, and then he shut the box and locked it away again for many months.

Whump! Whump! went the bass. *Tchg-tchg-tchga-tchg,* the gourds.

The gelatins splayed reds, greens, blues, and godawful yellows about the amazing metal dancers.

HUMAN? asked the marquee.

ROBOTS? (immediately below).

COME SEE FOR YOURSELF! (across the bottom, cryptically).

So they did.

Render and Jill were sitting at a microscopic table, thankfully set back against a wall, beneath charcoal caricatures of personalities largely unknown (there being so many personalities among the subcultures of a city of 14 million people). Nose crinkled with pleasure, Jill stared at the present focal point of this particular subculture, occasionally raising her shoulders to ear level to add emphasis to a silent laugh or a small squeal, because the performers were just *too* human—the way the ebon robot ran his fingers along the silver robot's forearm as they parted and passed. . . .

Render alternated his attention between Jill and the

dancers and a wicked-looking decoction that resembled
nothing so much as a small bucket of whisky sours
strewn with seaweed (through which the Kraken might
at any moment arise to drag some hapless ship down to
its doom).

"Charlie, I think they're really people!"

Render disentangled his gaze from her hair and
bouncing earrings.

He studied the dancers down on the floor, somewhat
below the table area, surrounded by music.

There *could* be humans within those metal shells. If
so, their dance was a thing of extreme skill. Though the
manufacture of sufficiently light alloys was no problem,
it would be some trick for a dancer to cavort so
freely—and for so long a period of time, and with such
effortless-seeming ease—within a head-to-toe suit of
armor, without so much as a grate or a click or a clank.

Soundless . . .

They glided like two gulls; the larger, the color of
polished anthracite, and the other, like a moonbeam
falling through a window upon a silk-wrapped manikin.

Even when they touched there was no sound—or if
there was, it was wholly masked by the rhythms of the
band.

Whump-whump! Tchga-tchg!

Render took another drink.

Slowly, it turned into an apache-dance. Render
checked his watch. Too long for normal entertainers, he
decided. They must be robots. As he looked up again the
black robot hurled the silver robot perhaps ten feet and
turned his back on her.

There was no sound of striking metal.

Wonder what a setup like that costs? he mused.

"Charlie! There was no sound! How do they do that?"

"I've no idea," said Render.

The gelatins were yellow again, then red, then blue,
then green.

"You'd think it would damage their mechanisms,
wouldn't you?"

The white robot crawled back and the other swiveled his wrist around and around, a lighted cigarette between the fingers. There was laughter as he pressed it mechanically to his lipless faceless face. The silver robot confronted him. He turned away again, dropped the cigarette, ground it out slowly, soundlessly, then suddenly turned back to his partner. Would he throw her again? No . . .

Slowly then, like the great-legged birds of the East, they recommenced their movement, slowly, and with many turnings away.

Something deep within Render was amused, but he was too far gone to ask it what was funny. So he went looking for the Kraken in the bottom of the glass instead.

Jill was clutching his bicep then, drawing his attention back to the floor.

As the spotlight tortured the spectrum, the black robot raised the silver one high above his head, slowly, slowly, and then commenced spinning with her in that position—arms outstretched, back arched, legs scissored—very slowly, at first. Then faster.

Suddenly they were whirling with an unbelievable speed, and the gelatins rotated faster and faster.

Render shook his head to clear it.

They were moving so rapidly that they *had* to fall—human or robot. But they didn't. They were a mandala. They were a gray form uniformity. Render looked down.

Then slowing, and slower, slower. Stopped.

The music stopped.

Blackness followed. Applause filled it.

When the lights came on again the two robots were standing statue-like, facing the audience. Very, very slowly, they bowed.

The applause increased.

Then they turned and were gone.

Then the music came on and the light was clear again. A babble of voices arose. Render slew the Kraken.

"What d'you think of that?" she asked him.

Render made his face serious and said: "Am I a man dreaming I am a robot, or a robot dreaming I am a man?" He grinned, then added: "I don't know."

She punched his shoulder gaily at that and he observed that she was drunk.

"I am not," she protested. "Not much, anyhow. Not as much as you."

"Still, I think you ought to see a doctor about it. Like me. Like now. Let's get out of here and go for a drive."

"Not yet, Charlie. I want to see them once more, huh? Please?"

"If I have another drink I won't be able to see that far."

"Then order a cup of coffee."

"Yaagh!"

"Then order a beer."

"I'll suffer without."

There were people on the dance floor now, but Render's feet felt like lead.

He lit a cigarette.

"So you had a dog talk to you today?"

"Yes. Something very disconcerting about that. . . ."

"Was she pretty?"

"It was a boy dog. And boy, was he ugly!"

"Silly. I mean his mistress."

"You know I never discuss cases, Jill."

"You told me about her being blind and about the dog. All I want to know is if she's pretty."

"Well . . . Yes and no." He bumped her under the table and gestured vaguely. "Well, you know . . ."

"Same thing all the way around," she told the waiter who had appeared suddenly out of an adjacent pool of darkness, nodded, and vanished as abruptly.

"There go my good intentions," sighed Render. "See how you like being examined by a drunken sot, that's all I can say."

"You'll sober up fast, you always do. Hippocratics and all that."

He sniffed, glanced at his watch.

"I have to be in Connecticut tomorrow. Pulling Pete out of that damned school. . . ."

She sighed, already tired of the subject.

"I think you worry too much about him. Any kid can bust an ankle. It's a part of growing up. I broke my wrist when I was seven. It was an accident. It's not the school's fault those things sometimes happen."

"Like hell," said Render, accepting his dark drink from the dark tray the dark man carried. "If they can't do a good job I'll find someone who can."

She shrugged.

"You're the boss. All I know is what I read in the papers.

"—And you're still set on Davos, even though you know you meet a better class of people at St. Moritz?" she added.

"We're going there to ski, remember? I like the runs better at Davos."

"I can't score any tonight, can I?"

He squeezed her hand.

"You always score with me, honey."

And they drank their drinks and smoked their cigarettes and held their hands until the people left the dance floor and filed back to their microscopic tables, and the gelatins spun round and round, tinting clouds of smoke from hell to sunrise and back again, and the bass went *whump!*

Tchga-tchga!

"Oh, Charlie! Here they come again!"

The sky was clear as crystal. The roads were clean. The snow had stopped.

Jill's breathing was the breathing of a sleeper. The S-7 raced across the bridges of the city. If Render sat very still he could convince himself that only his body was drunk; but whenever he moved his head the universe began to dance about him. As it did so, he imagined himself within a dream, and Shaper of it all.

For one instant this was true. He turned the big clock in the sky backward, smiling as he dozed. Another instant and he was awake again, and unsmiling.

The universe had taken revenge for his presumption. For one reknown moment with the helplessness which he had loved beyond helping, it had charged him the price of the lake-bottom vision once again; and as he had moved once more toward the wreck at the bottom of the world—like a swimmer, as unable to speak—he heard, from somewhere high over the Earth, and filtered down to him through the waters above the Earth, the howl of the Fenris Wolf as it prepared to devour the moon; and as this occurred, he knew that the sound was as like to the trump of a judgment as the lady by his side was unlike the moon. Every bit. In all ways. And he was afraid.

III

". . . The plain, the direct, and the blunt. This is Winchester Cathedral," said the guidebook. "With its floor-to-ceiling shafts, like so many huge treetrunks, it achieves a ruthless control over its spaces: the ceilings are flat; each bay, separated by those shafts, is itself a thing of certainty and stability. It seems, indeed, to reflect something of the spirit of William the Conqueror. Its disdain of mere elaboration and its passionate dedication to the love of another world would make it seem, too, an appropriate setting for some tale out of Mallory. . . ."

"Observe the scalloped capitals," said the guide. "In their primitive fluting they anticipated what was later to become a common motif. . . ."

"Faugh!" said Render—softly though, because he was in a group inside a church.

"Shh!" said Jill (Fotlock—that was her real last name) DeVille.

But Render was impressed as well as distressed.

Hating Jill's hobby though, had become so much of a reflex with him that he would sooner have taken his rest seated beneath an oriental device which dripped water on his head than to admit he occasionally enjoyed walking through the arcades and the galleries, the passages and the tunnels, and getting all out of breath climbing up the high twisty stairways of towers.

So he ran his eyes over everything, burnt everything down by shutting them, then built the place up again out of the still smouldering ashes of memory, all so that at a later date he would be able to repeat the performance, offering the vision to his one patient who could see only in this manner. This building he disliked less than most. Yes, he would take it back to her.

The camera in his mind photographing the surroundings, Render walked with the others, overcoat over his arm, his fingers anxious to reach after a cigarette. He kept busy ignoring his guide, realizing this to be the nadir of all forms of human protest. As he walked through Winchester he thought of his last two sessions with Eileen Shallot. He recalled his almost unwilling Adam-attitude as he had named all the animals passing before them, led of course by the *one* she had wanted to see, colored fearsome by his own unease. He had felt pleasantly bucolic after boning up on an old botany text and then proceeding to Shape and name the flowers of the fields.

So far they had stayed out of the cities, far away from the machines. Her emotions were still too powerful at the sight of the simple, carefully introduced objects to risk plunging her into so complicated and chaotic a wilderness yet; he would build her city slowly.

Something passed rapidly, high above the cathedral, uttering a sonic boom. Render took Jill's hand in his for a moment and smiled as she looked up at him. Knowing she verged upon beauty, Jill normally took great pains to achieve it. But today her hair was simply drawn back and knotted behind her head, and her lips and her eyes were pale; and her exposed ears were tiny and white and somewhat pointed.

"Observe the scalloped capitals," he whispered. "In their primitive fluting they anticipated what was later to become a common motif."

"Faugh!" said she.

"Shh!" said a sunburnt little woman nearby, whose face seemed to crack and fall back together again as she pursed and unpursed her lips.

Later, as they strolled back toward their hotel, Render said, "Okay on Winchester?"

"Okay on Winchester."

"Happy?"

"Happy."

"Good, then we can leave this afternoon."

"All right."

"For Switzerland. . . ."

She stopped and toyed with a button on his coat.

"Couldn't we just spend a day or two looking at some old chateaux first? After all, they're just across the Channel, and you could be sampling all the local wines while I looked . . ."

"Okay," he said.

She looked up—a trifle surprised.

"What? No argument?" she smiled. "Where is your fighting spirit?—to let me push you around like this?"

She took his arm then and they walked on as he said, "Yesterday, while we were galloping about in the innards of that old castle, I heard a weak moan, and then a voice cried out, 'For the love of God, Montresor!' I think it was my fighting spirit, because I'm certain it was my voice. I've given up *der geist der stets verneint. Pax vobiscum!* Let us be gone to France. *Alors!*"

"Dear Rendy, it'll only be another day or two. . . ."

"Amen," he said, "though my skis that were waxed are already waning."

So they did that, and on the morn of the third day, when she spoke to him of castles in Spain, he reflected aloud that while psychologists drink and only grow angry, psychiatrists have been known to drink, grow angry, and break things. Construing this as a veiled threat aimed at the Wedgwoods she had collected, she acquiesced to his desire to go skiing.

Free! Render almost screamed it.

His heart was pounding inside his head. He leaned hard. He cut to the left. The wind strapped at his face; a shower of ice crystals, like bullets of emery, fled by him, scraped against his cheek.

He was moving. Aye—the world had ended at

Weissflujoch, and Dorftali led down and away from this portal.

His feet were two gleaming rivers which raced across the stark, curving plains; they could not be frozen in their course. Downward. He flowed. Away from all the rooms of the world. Away from the stifling lack of intensity, from the day's hundred spoon-fed welfares, from the killing pace of the forced amusements that hacked at the Hydra, leisure; away.

And as he fled down the run he felt a strong desire to look back over his shoulder, as though to see whether the world he had left behind and above had set one fearsome embodiment of itself, like a shadow, to trail along after him, hunt him down and drag him back to a warm and well-lit coffin in the sky, there to be laid to rest with a spike of aluminum driven through his will and a garland of alternating currents smothering his spirit.

"I hate you," he breathed between clenched teeth, and the wind carried the words back; and he laughed then, for he always analyzed his emotions, as a matter of reflex; and he added, "Exit Orestes, mad, pursued by the Furies. . . ."

After a time the slope leveled out and he reached the bottom of the run and had to stop.

He smoked one cigarette then and rode back up to the top so that he could come down it again for non-therapeutic reasons.

That night he sat before a fire in the big lodge, feeling its warmth soaking into his tired muscles. Jill massaged his shoulders as he played Rorschach with the flames, and he came upon a blazing goblet which was snatched away from him in the same instant by the sound of his name being spoken somewhere across the Hall of the Nine Hearths.

"Charles Render!" said the voice (only it sounded more like "Sharlz Runder"), and his head instantly jerked in that direction, but his eyes danced with too many afterimages for him to isolate the source of the calling.

"Maurice?" he queried after a moment, "Bartelmetz?"

"Aye," came the reply, and then Render saw the familiar grizzled visage, set neckless and balding above the red and blue shag sweater that was stretched mercilessly about the wine-keg rotundity of the man who now picked his way in their direction, deftly avoiding the strewn crutches and the stacked skis and the people who, like Jill and Render, disdained sitting in chairs.

Render stood, stretching, and shook hands as he came upon them.

"You've put on more weight," Render observed. "That's unhealthy."

"Nonsense, it's all muscle. How have you been, and what are you up to these days?" He looked down at Jill and she smiled back at him.

"This is Miss DeVille," said Render.

"Jill," she acknowledged.

He bowed slightly, finally releasing Render's aching hand.

". . . And this is Professor Maurice Bartelmetz of Vienna," finished Render, "a benighted disciple of all forms of dialectical pessimism, and a very distinguished pioneer in neuroparticipation—although you'd never guess it to look at him. I had the good fortune to be his pupil for over a year."

Bartelmetz nodded and agreed with him, taking in the Schnappsflasche Render brought forth from a small plastic bag, and accepting the collapsible cup which he filled to the brim.

"Ah, you are a good doctor still," he sighed. "You have diagnosed the case in an instant and you make the proper prescription. Nozdrovia!"

"Seven years in a gulp," Render acknowledged, refilling their glasses.

"Then we shall make time more malleable by sipping it."

They seated themselves on the floor, and the fire roared up through the great brick chimney as the logs burnt themselves back to branches, to twigs, to thin sticks, ring by yearly ring.

Render replenished the fire.

"I read your last book," said Bartelmetz finally, casually, "about four years ago."

Render reckoned that to be correct.

"Are you doing any research work these days?"

Render poked lazily at the fire.

"Yes," he answered, "sort of."

He glanced at Jill, who was dozing with her cheek against the arm of the huge leather chair that held his emergency bag, the planes of her face all crimson and flickering shadow.

"I've hit upon a rather unusual subject and started with a piece of jobbery I eventually intend to write about."

"Unusual? In what way?"

"Blind from birth, for one thing."

"You're using the ONT&R?"

"Yes. She's going to be a Shaper."

"Verfluchter!—Are you aware of the possible repercussions?"

"Of course."

"You've heard of unlucky Pierre?"

"No."

"Good, then it was successfully hushed. Pierre was a philosophy student at the University of Paris, and was doing a dissertation on the evolution of consciousness. This past summer he decided it would be necessary for him to explore the mind of an ape, for purposes of comparing a moins-nausée mind with his own, I suppose. At any rate, he obtained illegal access to an ONT&R and to the mind of our hairy cousin. It was never ascertained how far along he got in exposing the animal to the stimuli-bank, but it is to be assumed that such items as would not be immediately trans-subjective between man and ape—traffic sounds and so weiter—

were what frightened the creature. Pierre is still residing in a padded cell, and all his responses are those of a
frightened ape.

"So, while he did not complete his own dissertation,"
he finished, "he may provide significant material for
someone else's."

Render shook his head.

"Quite a story," he said softly, "but I have nothing
that dramatic to contend with. I've found an exceeding-
ly stable individual—a psychiatrist, in fact—one who's
already spent time in ordinary analysis. She wants to go
into neuroparticipation—but the fear of a sight-trauma
was what was keeping her out. I've been gradually
exposing her to a full range of visual phenomena. When
I've finished she should be completely accommodated
to sight, so that she can give her full attention to therapy
and not be blinded by vision, so to speak. We've already
had four sessions."

"And?"

". . . And it's working fine."

"You are certain about it?"

"Yes, as certain as anyone can be in these matters."

"Mm-hm," said Bartelmetz. "Tell me, do you find her
excessively strong-willed? By that I mean, say, perhaps
an obsessive-compulsive pattern concerning anything to
which she's been introduced so far?"

"No."

"Has she ever succeeded in taking over control of the
fantasy?"

"No!"

"You lie," he said simply.

Render found a cigarette. After lighting it, he smiled.

"Old father, old artificer," he conceded, "age has not
withered your perceptiveness. I may trick me, but never
you.—Yes, as a matter of fact, she *is* very difficult to
keep under control. She is not satisfied just to see. She
wants to Shape things for herself already. It's quite
understandable—both to her and to me—but conscious apprehension and emotional acceptance never

do seem to get together on things. She has become dominant on several occasions, but I've succeeded in resuming control almost immediately. After all, I *am* master of the bank."

"Hm," mused Bartelmetz. "Are you familiar with a Buddhist text—*Shankara's Catechism*?"

"I'm afraid not."

"Then I lecture you on it now. It posits—obviously not for therapeutic purposes—a true ego and a false ego. The true ego is that part of man which is immortal and shall proceed on to nirvana: the soul, if you like. Very good. Well, the false ego, on the other hand, is the normal mind, bound round with the illusions—the consciousness of you and me and everyone we have ever known professionally. Good?—Good. Now, the stuff this false ego is made up of they call skandhas. These include the feelings, the perceptions, the aptitudes, consciousness itself, and even the physical form. Very unscientific. Yes. Now they are not the same thing as neuroses, or one of Mister Ibsen's life-lies, or an hallucination—no, even though they are all wrong, being parts of a false thing to begin with. Each of the five skandhas is a part of the eccentricity that we call identity—then on top come the neuroses and all the other messes which follow after and keep us in business. Okay?—Okay. I give you this lecture because I need a dramatic term for what I will say, because I wish to say something dramatic. View the skandhas as lying at the bottom of the pond; the neuroses, they are ripples on the top of the water; the 'true ego,' if there is one, is buried deep beneath the sand at the bottom. So. The ripples fill up the—the—zwischenwelt—between the object and the subject. The skandhas are a part of the subject, basic, unique, the stuff of his being.—So far, you are with me?"

"With many reservations."

"Good. Now I have defined my term somewhat, I will use it. You are fooling around with skandhas, not simple neuroses. You are attempting to adjust this woman's overall conception of herself and of the world. You are using the ONT&R to do it. It is the same thing as fooling with a psychotic or an ape. All may seem to go well, but—at any moment, it is possible you may do something, show her some sight, or some way of seeing which will break in upon her selfhood, break a skandha—and pouf!—it will be like breaking through the bottom of the pond. A whirlpool will result, pulling you—where? I do not want you for a patient, young man, young artificer, so I counsel you not to proceed with this experiment. The ONT&R should not be used in such a manner."

Render flipped his cigarette into the fire and counted on his fingers:

"One," he said, "you are making a mystical mountain out of a pebble. All I am doing is adjusting her consciousness to accept an additional area of perception. Much of it is simple transference work from the other senses— Two, her emotions were quite intense initially because it *did* involve a trauma—but we've passed that stage already. Now it is only a novelty to her. Soon it will be a commonplace— Three, Eileen is a psychiatrist herself; she is educated in these matters and deeply aware of the delicate nature of what we are doing— Four, her sense of identity and her desires, or her skandhas, or whatever you want to call them, are as firm as the Rock of Gibraltar. Do you realize the intense application required for a blind person to obtain the education she has obtained? It took a will of ten-point steel and the emotional control of an ascetic as well—"

"—And if something that strong should break, in a timeless moment of anxiety," smiled Bartelmetz sadly, "may the shades of Sigmund Freud and Carl Jung walk by your side in the valley of darkness.

"—And five," he added suddenly, staring into Render's eyes. "Five," he ticked it off on one finger. "Is she pretty?"

Render looked back into the fire.

"Very clever," sighed Bartelmetz, "I cannot tell

whether you are blushing or not, with the rosy glow of the flames upon your face. I fear that you are, though, which would mean that you are aware that you yourself could be the source of the inciting stimulus. I shall burn a candle tonight before a portrait of Adler and pray that he give you the strength to compete successfully in your duel with your patient.''

Render looked at Jill, who was still sleeping. He reached out and brushed a lock of her hair back into place.

"Still," said Bartelmetz, "if you do proceed and all goes well, I shall look forward with great interest to the reading of your work. Did I ever tell you that I have treated several Buddhists and never found a 'true ego'?"

Both men laughed.

Like me but not like me, that one on a leash, smelling of fear, small, gray, and unseeing. *Rrowl* and he'll choke on his collar. His head is empty as the oven till She pushes the button and it makes dinner. Make talk and they never understand, but they are like me. One day I will kill one—why? . . . Turn here.

"Three steps. Up. Glass doors. Handle to right."

Why? Ahead, drop-shaft. Gardens under, down. Smells nice, there. Grass, wet dirt, trees, and clean air. I see. Birds are recorded though. I see all. I.

"Drop-shaft. Four steps."

Down. Yes. Want to make loud noises in throat, feel silly. Clean, smooth, many of trees. God . . . She likes sitting on bench chewing leaves smelling smooth air. Can't see them like me. Maybe now, some . . . ? No.

Can't Bad Sigmund me on grass, trees, here. Must hold it. Pity. Best place . . .

"Watch for steps."

Ahead. To right, to left, to right, to left, trees and grass now. Sigmund sees. Walking . . . Doctor with machine gives her his eyes. *Rrowl* and he will not choke. No fearsmell.

Dig deep hole in ground, bury eyes. God is blind. Sigmund to see. Her eyes now filled, and he is afraid of teeth. Will make her to see and take her high up in the sky to see, away. Leave me here, leave Sigmund with none to see, alone. I will dig a deep hole in the ground . . .

It was after ten in the morning when Jill awoke. She did not have to turn her head to know that Render was already gone. He never slept late. She rubbed her eyes, stretched, turned onto her side and raised herself on her elbow. She squinted at the clock on the bedside table, simultaneously reaching for a cigarette and her lighter.

As she inhaled, she realized there was no ashtray. Doubtless Render had moved it to the dresser because he did not approve of smoking in bed. With a sigh that ended in a snort she slid out of the bed and drew on her wrap before the ash grew too long.

She hated getting up, but once she did she would permit the day to begin and continue on without lapse through its orderly progression of events.

"Damn him," she smiled. She had wanted her breakfast in bed, but it was too late now.

Between thoughts as to what she would wear, she observed an alien pair of skis standing in the corner. A sheet of paper was impaled on one. She approached it.

"Join me?" asked the scrawl.

She shook her head in an emphatic negative and felt somewhat sad. She had been on skis twice in her life and she was afraid of them. She felt that she should really try again, after his being a reasonably good sport about the chateaux, but she could not even bear the memory of the unseemly downward rushing—which, on two occasions, had promptly deposited her in a snowbank—without wincing and feeling once again the vertigo that had seized her during the attempts.

So she showered and dressed and went downstairs for breakfast.

All nine fires were already roaring as she passed the big hall and looked inside. Some red-faced skiers were holding their hands up before the blaze of the central hearth. It was not crowded though. The racks held only a few pairs of dripping boots, bright caps hung on pegs, moist skis stood upright in their place beside the door. A few people were seated in the chairs set further back toward the center of the hall, reading papers, smoking, or talking quietly. She saw no one she knew, so she moved on toward the dining room.

As she passed the registration desk the old man who worked there called out her name. She approached him and smiled.

"Letter," he explained, turning to a rack. "Here it is," he announced, handing it to her. "Looks important."

It had been forwarded three times, she noted. It was a bulky brown envelope, and the return address was that of her attorney.

"Thank you."

She moved off to a seat beside the big window that looked out upon a snow garden, a skating rink, and a distant winding trail dotted with figures carrying skis over their shoulders. She squinted against the brightness as she tore open the envelope.

Yes, it was final. Her attorney's note was accompanied by a copy of the divorce decree. She had only recently decided to end her legal relationship to Mister Fotlock, whose name she had stopped using five years earlier, when they had separated. Now that she had the thing she wasn't sure exactly what she was going to do with it. It would be a hell of a surprise for dear Rendy, though, she decided. She would have to find a reasonably innocent way of getting the information to him. She withdrew her compact and practiced a "Well?" expression. Well, there would be time for that later, she mused. Not too much later, though . . . Her thirtieth birthday, like a huge black cloud, filled an April but four months distant. Well . . . She touched her quizzical lips with color, dusted more powder over her mole, and locked the expression within her compact for future use.

In the dining room she saw Doctor Bartelmetz, seated before an enormous mound of scrambled eggs, great chains of dark sausages, several heaps of yellow toast, and a half-emptied flask of orange juice. A pot of coffee steamed on the warmer at his elbow. He leaned slightly forward as he ate, wielding his fork like a windmill blade.

"Good morning," she said.

He looked up.

"Miss DeVille—Jill . . . Good morning." He nodded at the chair across from him. "Join me, please."

She did so, and when the waiter approached she nodded and said, "I'll have the same thing, only about ninety percent less."

She turned back to Bartelmetz.

"Have you seen Charles today?"

"Alas, I have not," he gestured, open-handed, "and I wanted to continue our discussion while his mind was still in the early stages of wakefulness and somewhat malleable. Unfortunately," he took a sip of coffee, "he who sleeps well enters the day somewhere in the middle of its second act."

"Myself, I usually come in around intermission and ask someone for a synopsis," she explained. "So why not continue the discussion with me?—I'm always malleable, and my skandhas are in good shape."

Their eyes met, and he took a bite of toast.

"Aye," he said, at length, "I had guessed as much. Well—good. What do you know of Render's work?"

She adjusted herself in the chair.

"Mm. He being a special specialist in a highly specialized area, I find it difficult to appreciate the few things he does say about it. I'd like to be able to look inside other people's minds sometimes—to see what they're thinking about *me*, of course—but I don't think I could stand staying there very long. Especially," she gave a mock-shudder, "the mind of somebody with— problems. I'm afraid I'd be too sympathetic or too frightened or something. Then, according to what I've read—pow!—like sympathetic magic, it would be my problem.

"Charles never has problems though," she continued, "at least, none that he speaks to me about. Lately I've been wondering, though. That blind girl and her talking dog seem to be too much with him."

"Talking dog?"

"Yes, her Seeing Eye dog is one of those surgical mutants."

"How interesting. . . . Have you ever met her?"

"Never."

"So," he mused.

"Sometimes a therapist encounters a patient whose problems are so akin to his own that the sessions become extremely mordant," he noted. "It has always been the case with me when I treat a fellow-psychiatrist. Perhaps Charles sees in this situation a parallel to something which has been troubling him personally. I did not administer his personal analysis. I do not know all the ways of his mind, even though he was a pupil of mine for a long while. He was always self-contained, somewhat reticent; he could be quite authoritative on occasion, however.—What are some of the other things which occupy his attention these days?"

"His son Peter is a constant concern. He's changed the boy's school five times in five years."

Her breakfast arrived. She adjusted her napkin and drew her chair closer to the table.

"And he has been reading case histories of suicides recently, and talking about them, and talking about them, and talking about them."

"To what end?"

She shrugged and began eating.

"He never mentioned why," she said, looking up again. "Maybe he's writing something. . . ."

Bartelmetz finished his eggs and poured more coffee.

"Are you afraid of this patient of his?" he inquired.

"No . . . Yes," she responded, "I am."

"Why?"

"I am afraid of sympathetic magic," she said, flushing slightly.

"Many things could fall under that heading."

"Many indeed," she acknowledged. And, after a moment, "We are united in our concern for his welfare and in agreement as to what represents the threat. So, may I ask a favor?"

"You may."

"Talk to him again," she said. "Persuade him to drop the case."

He folded his napkin.

"I intend to do that after dinner," he stated, "because I believe in the ritualistic value of rescue-motions. They shall be made."

Dear Father-Image,

Yes, the school is fine, my ankle is getting that way, and my classmates are a congenial lot. No, I am not short on cash, undernourished, or having difficulty fitting into the new curriculum. Okay?

The building I will not describe, as you have already seen the macabre thing. The grounds I cannot describe, as they are presently residing beneath cold white sheets. Brr! I trust yourself to be enjoying the arts wint'rish. I do not share your enthusiasm for summer's opposite, except within picture frames or as an emblem on ice cream bars.

The ankle inhibits my mobility and my roommate has gone home for the weekend—both of which are really blessings (saith Pangloss), for I now have the opportunity to catch up on some reading. I will do so forthwith.

                                        Prodigally,
                                        Peter

Render reached down to pat the huge head. It accepted the gesture stoically, then turned its gaze up to the Austrian whom Render had asked for a light, as if to say, "Must I endure this indignity?" The man laughed at the expression, snapping shut the engraved lighter on which Render noted the middle initial to be a small 'v.'

"Thank you," he said, and to the dog: "What is your name?"

"Bismark," it growled.

Render smiled.

"You remind me of another of your kind," he told the dog. "One Sigmund, by name, a companion and guide to a blind friend of mine, in America."

"My Bismark is a hunter," said the young man. "There is no quarry that can outthink him, neither the deer nor the big cats."

The dog's ears pricked forward and he stared up at Render with proud, blazing eyes.

"We have hunted in Africa and the northern and southwestern parts of America. Central America, too. He never loses the trail. He never gives up. He is a beautiful brute, and his teeth could have been made in Solingen."

"You are indeed fortunate to have such a hunting companion."

"I hunt," growled the dog. "I follow . . . Sometimes, I have, the kill . . ."

"You would not know of the one called Sigmund then, or the woman he guides—Miss Eileen Shallot?" asked Render.

The man shook his head.

"No, Bismark came to me from Massachusetts, but I was never to the Center personally. I am not acquainted with other mutie handlers."

"I see. Well, thank you for the light. Good afternoon."

"Good afternoon . . ."

"Good, after, noon . . ."

Render strolled on up the narrow street, hands in his

pockets. He had excused himself and not said where he was going. This was because he had had no destination in mind. Bartelmetz' second essay at counseling had almost led him to say things he would later regret. It was easier to take a walk than to continue the conversation.

On a sudden impulse he entered a small shop and bought a cuckoo clock which had caught his eye. He felt certain that Bartelmetz would accept the gift in the proper spirit. He smiled and walked on. *And what was that letter to Jill which the desk clerk had made a special trip to their table to deliver at dinnertime?* he wondered. It had been forwarded three times, and its return address was that of a law firm. Jill had not even opened it, but had smiled, overtipped the old man, and tucked it into her purse. He would have to hint subtly as to its contents. His curiosity was so aroused that she would be sure to tell him out of pity.

The icy pillars of the sky suddenly seemed to sway before him as a cold wind leapt down out of the north. Render hunched his shoulders and drew his head further below his collar. Clutching the cuckoo clock, he hurried back up the street.

That night the serpent which holds its tail in its mouth belched, the Fenris Wolf made a pass at the moon, the little clock said "cuckoo," and tomorrow came on like Manolete's last bull, shaking the gate of horn with the bellowed promise to tread a river of lions to sand.

Render promised himself he would lay off the gooey fondue.

Later, much later, when they skipped through the skies in a kite-shaped cruiser, Render looked down upon the darkened Earth dreaming its cities full of stars, looked up at the sky where they were all reflected, looked about him at the tape-screens watching all the people who blinked into them, and at the coffee, tea, and mixed drink dispensers who sent their fluids forth to explore the insides of the people they required to push their buttons, then looked across at Jill, whom the old buildings had compelled to walk among their walls —because he knew she felt he should be looking at her then—felt his seat's demand that he convert it into a couch, did so, and slept.

IV

Her office was full of flowers, and she liked exotic perfumes. Sometimes she burned incense.

She liked soaking in overheated pools, walking through falling snow, listening to too much music, played perhaps too loudly, drinking five or six varieties of liqueurs (usually reeking of anise, sometimes touched with wormwood) every evening. Her hands were soft and lightly freckled. Her fingers were long and tapered. She wore no rings.

Her fingers traced and retraced the floral swellings on the side of her chair as she spoke into the recording unit:

". . . Patient's chief complaints on admission were nervousness, insomnia, stomach pains, and a period of depression. Patient has had a record of previous admissions for short periods of time. He had been in this hospital in 1995 for a manic depressive psychosis, depressed type, and he returned here again, 2-3-96. He was in another hospital, 9-20-97. Physical examination revealed a BP of 170/100. He was normally developed and well-nourished on the date of examination, 12-11-98. On this date patient complained of chronic backache, and there was noted some moderate symptoms of alcohol withdrawal. Physical examination further revealed no pathology except that the patient's tendon reflexes were exaggerated but equal. These symptoms were the result of alcohol withdrawal. Upon admission he was shown to be not psychotic, neither delusional nor hallucinated. He was well-oriented as to place, time, and person. His psychological condition was evaluated and he was found to be somewhat grandiose and expansive and more than a little hostile. He was considered a potential troublemaker. Because of his experience as a cook, he was assigned to work in the kitchen. His general condition then showed definite improvement. He is less tense and is cooperative. Diagnosis: Manic depressive reaction (external precipitating stress unknown). The degree of psychiatric impairment is mild. He is considered competent. To be continued on therapy and hospitalization."

She turned off the recorder then and laughed. The sound frightened her. Laughter is a social phenomenon and she was alone. She played back the recording then, chewing on the corner of her handkerchief while the soft, clipped words were returned to her. She ceased to hear them after the first dozen or so.

When the recorder stopped talking she turned it off. She was alone. She was very alone. She was so damned alone that the little pool of brightness which occurred when she stroked her forehead and faced the window—that little pool of brightness suddenly became the most important thing in the world. She wanted it to be immense. She wanted it to be an ocean of light. Or else she wanted to grow so small herself that the effect would be the same: she wanted to drown in it.

It had been three weeks, yesterday . . .

Too long, she decided, *I should have waited. No! Impossible! But what if he goes as Riscomb went? No! He won't. He would not. Nothing can hurt him. Never. He is all strength and armor. But—but we should have waited till next month to start. Three weeks . . . Sight withdrawal —that's what it is. Are the memories fading? Are they weaker? What does a tree look like? Or a cloud?—I can't remember! What is red? What is green? God! It's hysterical! I'm watching and I can't stop it!—Take a pill! A pill!*

Her shoulders began to shake. She did not take a pill

though, but bit down harder on the handkerchief until her sharp teeth tore through its fabric.

"Beware," she recited a personal beatitude, "those who hunger and thirst after justice, for we *will* be satisfied.

"And beware the meek," she continued, "for we shall attempt to inherit the Earth.

"And beware . . ."

There was a brief buzz from the phone-box. She put away her handkerchief, composed her face, turned the unit on.

"Hello . . . ?"

"Eileen, I'm back. How've you been?"

"Good, quite well in fact. How was your vacation?"

"Oh, I can't complain. I had it coming for a long time. I guess I deserve it. Listen, I brought some things back to show you—like Winchester Cathedral. You want to come in this week? I can make it any evening."

Tonight. No. I want it too badly. It will set me back if he sees . . .

"How about tomorrow night?" she asked. "Or the one after?"

"Tomorrow will be fine," he said. "Meet you at the P & S, around seven?"

"Yes, that would be pleasant. Same table?"

"Why not?—I'll reserve it."

"All right. I'll see you then."

"Goodbye."

The connection was broken.

Suddenly, then, at that moment, colors swirled again through her head; and she saw trees—oaks and pines, poplars and sycamores—great, and green and brown, and iron-colored; and she saw wads of fleecy clouds, dipped in paintpots, swabbing a pastel sky; and a burning sun, and a small willow tree, and a lake of a deep, almost violet, blue. She folded her torn handkerchief and put it away.

She pushed a button beside her desk and music filled the office: Scriabin. Then she pushed another button and replayed the tape she had dictated, half-listening to each.

Pierre sniffed suspiciously at the food. The attendant moved away from the tray and stepped out into the hall, locking the door behind him. The enormous salad waited on the floor. Pierre approached cautiously, snatched a handful of lettuce, gulped it.

He was afraid.

If only the steel would stop crashing and crashing against steel, somewhere in that dark night . . . If only . . .

Sigmund rose to his feet, yawned, stretched. His hind legs trailed out behind him for a moment, then he snapped to attention and shook himself. She would be coming home soon. Wagging his tail slowly, he glanced up at the human-level clock with the raised numerals, verified his feelings, then crossed the apartment to the teevee. He rose onto his hind legs, rested one paw against the table, and used the other to turn on the set.

It was nearly time for the weather report and the roads would be icy.

"I have driven through county-wide graveyards," wrote Render, "vast forests of stone that spread further every day.

"Why does man so zealously guard his dead? Is it because this is the monumentally democratic way of immortalization, the ultimate affirmation of the power to hurt—that is to say, life—and the desire that it continue on forever? Unamuno has suggested that this is the case. If it is, then a greater percentage of the population actively sought immortality last year than ever before in history. . . ."

* * *

Tch-tchg, tchga-tchg!
  "Do you think they're really people?"
  "Naw, they're too good."

The evening was starglint and soda over ice. Render
wound the S-7 into the cold sub-subcellar, found his
parking place, nosed into it.

There was a damp chill that emerged from the
concrete to gnaw like rats' teeth at their flesh. Render
guided her toward the lift, their breath preceding them
in dissolving clouds.

"A bit of a chill in the air," he noted.

She nodded, biting her lip.

Inside the lift, he sighed, unwound his scarf, lit a
cigarette.

"Give me one, please," she requested, smelling the
tobacco.

He did.

They rose slowly, and Render leaned against the wall,
puffing a mixture of smoke and crystallized moisture.

"I met another mutie shep," he recalled, "in Switzerland. Big as Sigmund. A hunter though, and as Prussian
as they come," he grinned.

"Sigmund likes to hunt, too," she observed. "Twice
every year we go up to the North Woods and I turn him
loose. He's gone for days at a time, and he's always quite
happy when he returns. Never says what he's done, but
he's never hungry. Back when I got him I guessed that
he would need vacations from humanity to stay stable. I
think I was right."

The lift stopped, the door opened, and they walked
out into the hall, Render guiding her again.

Inside his office, he poked at the thermostat and
warm air sighed through the room. He hung their coats
in the inner office and brought the great egg out from its
nest behind the wall. He connected it to an outlet and
moved to convert his desk into a control panel.

"How long do you think it will take?" she asked,
running her fingertips over the smooth, cold curves of

the egg. "The whole thing, I mean. The entire adaptation to seeing."

He wondered.

"I have no idea," he said, "no idea whatsoever, yet. We got off to a good start, but there's still a lot of work to be done. I think I'll be able to make a good guess in another three months."

She nodded wistfully, moved to his desk, explored the controls with fingerstrokes like ten feathers.

"Careful you don't push any of those."

"I won't. How long do you think it will take me to learn to operate one?"

"Three months to learn it. Six, to actually become proficient enough to use it on anyone; and an additional six under close supervision before you can be trusted on your own. —About a year altogether."

"Uh-huh." She chose a chair.

Render touched the seasons to life, and the phases of day and night, the breath of the country, the city, the elements that raced naked through the skies, and all the dozens of dancing cues he used to build worlds. He smashed the clock of time and tasted the seven or so ages of man.

"Okay," he turned, "everything is ready."

It came quickly, and with a minimum of suggestion on Render's part. One moment there was grayness. Then a dead-white fog. Then it broke itself apart, as though a quick wind had arisen, although he neither heard nor felt a wind.

He stood beside the willow tree beside the lake, and she stood half-hidden among the branches and the lattices of shadow. The sun was slanting its way into evening.

"We have come back," she said, stepping out, leaves in her hair. "For a time I was afraid it had never happened, but I see it all again, and I remember now."

"Good," he said. "Behold yourself." And she looked into the lake.

"I have not changed," she said. "I haven't changed. . . ."

"No."

"But you have," she continued, looking up at him. "You are taller, and there is something different. . . ."

"No," he answered.

"I am mistaken," she said quickly, "I don't understand everything I see yet. I will, though."

"Of course."

"What are we going to do?"

"Watch," he instructed her.

Along a flat, no-colored river of road she just then noticed beyond the trees, came the car. It came from the farthest quarter of the sky, skipping over the mountains, buzzing down the hills, circling through the glades, and splashing them with the colors of its voice—the gray and the silver of synchronized potency—and the lake shivered from its sounds, and the car stopped a hundred feet away, masked by the shrubberies; and it waited. It was the S-7.

"Come with me," he said, taking her hand. "We're going for a ride."

They walked among the trees and rounded the final cluster of bushes. She touched the sleek cocoon, its antennae, its tires, its windows—and the windows transpared as she did so. She stared through them at the inside of the car, and she nodded.

"It is your Spinner."

"Yes." He held the door for her. "Get in. We'll return to the club. The time is now. The memories are fresh, and they should be reasonably pleasant, or neutral."

"Pleasant," she said, getting in.

He closed the door, then circled the car and entered. She watched as he punched imaginary coordinates. The car leapt ahead and he kept a steady stream of trees flowing by them. He could feel the rising tension, so he did not vary the scenery. She swiveled her seat and studied the interior of the car.

"Yes," she finally said, "I can perceive what everything is."

She stared out the window again. She looked at the rushing trees. Render stared out and looked upon rushing anxiety patterns. He opaqued the windows.

"Good," she said, "thank you. Suddenly it was too much to see—all of it, moving past like a . . ."

"Of course," said Render, maintaining the sensations of forward motion. "I'd anticipated that. You're getting tougher, though."

After a moment, "Relax," he said, "relax now," and somewhere a button was pushed, and she relaxed, and they drove on, and on and on, and finally the car began to slow, and Render said, "Just for one nice, slow glimpse now, look out your window."

She did.

He drew upon every stimulus in the bank which could promote sensations of pleasure and relaxation, and he dropped the city around the car, and the windows became transparent, and she looked out upon the profiles of towers and a block of monolithic apartments, and then she saw three rapid cafeterias, an entertainment palace, a drugstore, a medical center of yellow brick with an aluminum caduceus set above its archway, and a glassed-in high school, now emptied of its pupils, a fifty-pump gas station, another drugstore, and many more cars, parked or roaring by them, and people, people moving in and out of the doorways and walking before the buildings and getting into the cars and getting out of the cars; and it was summer, and the light of late afternoon filtered down upon the colors of the city and the colors of the garments the people wore as they moved along the boulevard, as they loafed upon the terraces, as they crossed the balconies, leaned on balustrades and windowsills, emerged from a corner kiosk, entered one, stood talking to one another; a woman walking a poodle rounded a corner; rockets went to and fro in the high sky.

The world fell apart then and Render caught the pieces.

He maintained an absolute blackness, blanketing every sensation but that of their movement forward.

After a time a dim light occurred, and they were still seated in the Spinner, windows blanked again, and the air as they breathed it became a soothing unguent.

"Lord," she said, "the world is so filled. Did I really see all of that?"

"I wasn't going to do that tonight, but you wanted me to. You seemed ready."

"Yes," she said, and the windows became transparent again. She turned away quickly.

"It's gone," he said. "I only wanted to give you a glimpse."

She looked, and it was dark outside now, and they were crossing over a high bridge. They were moving slowly. There was no other traffic. Below them were the Flats, where an occasional smelter flared like a tiny, drowsing volcano, spitting showers of orange sparks skyward; and there were many stars: they glistened on the breathing water that went beneath the bridge; they silhouetted by pinprick the skyline that hovered dimly below its surface. The slanting struts of the bridge marched steadily by.

"You have done it," she said, "and I thank you." Then: "Who are you, really?" (He must have wanted her to ask that.)

"I am Render," he laughed. And they wound their way through a dark, now-vacant city, coming at last to their club and entering the great parking dome.

Inside, he scrutinized all her feelings, ready to banish the world at a moment's notice. He did not feel he would have to, though.

They left the car, moved ahead. They passed into the club, which he had decided would not be crowded tonight. They were shown to their table at the foot of the bar in the small room with the suit of armor, and they sat down and ordered the same meal over again.

"No," he said, looking down, "it belongs over there."

The suit of armor appeared once again beside the table, and he was once again inside his gray suit and black tie and silver tie clasp shaped like a tree limb.

They laughed.

"I'm just not the type to wear a tin suit, so I wish you'd stop seeing me that way."

"I'm sorry," she smiled. "I don't know how I did that, or why."

"I do, and I decline the nomination. Also, I caution you once again. You are conscious of the fact that this is all an illusion. I had to do it that way for you to get the full benefit of the thing. For most of my patients though, it is the real item while they are experiencing it. It makes a counter-trauma or a symbolic sequence even more powerful. You are aware of the parameters of the game, however, and whether you want it or not this gives you a different sort of control over it than I normally have to deal with. Please be careful."

"I'm sorry. I didn't mean to."

"I know. Here comes the meal we just had."

"Ugh! It looks dreadful! Did we eat all that stuff?"

"Yes," he chuckled. "That's a knife, that's a fork, that's a spoon. That's roast beef, and those are mashed potatoes, those are peas, that's butter . . ."

"Goodness! I don't feel so well."

". . . And those are the salads, and those are the salad dressings. This is a brook trout—mm! These are French fried potatoes. This is a bottle of wine. Hmm—let's see—Romanée-Conti, since I'm not paying for it—and a bottle of Yquem for the trou—Hey!"

The room was wavering.

He bared the table, he banished the restaurant. They were back in the glade. Through the transparent fabric of the world he watched a hand moving along a panel. Buttons were being pushed. The world grew substantial again. Their emptied table was set beside the lake now, and it was still nighttime and summer, and the tablecloth was very white under the glow of the giant moon that hung overhead.

"That was stupid of me," he said. "Awfully stupid. I should have introduced them one at a time. The actual sight of basic, oral stimuli can be very distressing to a person seeing them for the first time. I got so wrapped up in the Shaping that I forgot the patient, which is just dandy! I apologize."

"I'm okay now. Really I am."

He summoned a cool breeze from the lake.

". . . And that is the moon," he added lamely.

She nodded, and she was wearing a tiny moon in the center of her forehead; it glowed like the one above them, and her hair and dress were all of silver.

The bottle of Romanée-Conti stood on the table, and two glasses.

"Where did that come from?"

She shrugged. He poured out a glassful.

"It may taste kind of flat," he said.

"It doesn't. Here—" She passed it to him.

As he sipped it he realized it had a taste—a *fruite* such as might be quashed from the grapes grown in the Isles of the Blest, a smooth, muscular *charnu*, and a *capiteux* centrifuged from the fumes of a field of burning poppies. With a start, he knew that his hand must be traversing the route of the perceptions, symphonizing the sensual cues of a transference and a counter-transference which had come upon him all unawares, there beside the lake.

"So it does," he noted, "and now it is time we returned."

"So soon? I haven't seen the cathedral yet. . . ."

"So soon."

He willed the world to end, and it did.

"It is cold out there," she said as she dressed, "and dark."

"I know. I'll mix us something to drink while I clear the unit."

"Fine."

He glanced at the tapes and shook his head. He crossed to his bar cabinet.

"It's not exactly Romanée-Conti," he observed, reaching for a bottle.

"So what? I don't mind."

Neither did he, at that moment. So he cleared the unit, they drank their drinks, and he helped her into her coat and they left.

As they rode the lift down to the sub-sub he willed the world to end again, but it didn't.

Dad,

I hobbled from school to taxi and taxi to spaceport, for the local Air Force Exhibit—Outward, it was called. (Okay, I exaggerated the hobble. It got me extra attention though.) The whole bit was aimed at seducing young manhood into a five-year hitch, as I saw it. But it worked. I wanna join up. I wanna go Out There. Think they'll take me when I'm old enuff? I mean take me Out—not some crummy desk job. Think so?

I do.

There was this dam lite colonel ('scuse the French) who saw this kid lurching around and pressing his nose 'gainst the big windowpanes, and he decided to give him the subliminal sell. Great! He pushed me through the gallery and showed me all the pitchers of AF triumphs, from Moonbase to Marsport. He lectured me on the Great Traditions of the Service, and marched me into a flic room where the Corps had good clean fun on tape, wrestling one another in null-G "where it's all skill and no brawn," and making tinted water sculpture-work way in the middle of the air and doing dismounted drill on the skin of a cruiser. Oh joy!

Seriously though, I'd like to be there when they hit the Outer Five—and On Out. Not because of the bogus balonus in the throwaways, and suchlike crud, but because I think someone of sensibility should be along to chronicle the thing in the proper way. You know, raw frontier observer. Francis Parkman. Mary Austin, like that. So I decided I'm going.

The AF boy with the chicken stuff on his shoulders wasn't in the least way patronizing, gods be praised. We stood on the balcony and watched ships lift off and he told me to go forth and study real hard and I might be riding them some day. I did not bother to tell him that I'm hardly intellectually deficient and that I'll have my B.A. before I'm old enough to do anything with it, even join his Corps. I just watched the ships lift off and said, "Ten years from now I'll be looking down, not up." Then he told me how hard his own training had been, so I did not ask howcum he got stuck with a lousy dirtside assignment like this one. Glad I didn't, now I think on it. He looked more like one of their ads than one of their real people. Hope I never look like an ad.

Thank you for the monies and the warm sox and Mozart's String Quintets, which I'm hearing right now. I wanna put in my bid for Luna instead of Europe next summer. Maybe . . . ? Possibly . . . ? Contingently . . . ? Huh?—If I can smash that new test you're designing for me . . . ? Anyhow, please think about it.

> Your son,
> Pete

"Hello. State Psychiatric Institute."

"I'd like to make an appointment for an examination."

"Just a moment. I'll connect you with the Appointment Desk."

"Hello. Appointment Desk."

"I'd like to make an appointment for an examination."

"Just a moment . . . What sort of examination?"

"I want to see Doctor Shallot, Eileen Shallot. As soon as possible."

"Just a moment. I'll have to check her schedule . . . Could you make it at two o'clock next Tuesday?"

"That would be just fine."

"What is the name, please?"

"DeVille. Jill DeVille."

"All right, Miss DeVille. That's two o'clock, Tuesday."

"Thank you."

The man walked beside the highway. Cars passed along the highway. The cars in the high-acceleration lane blurred by.

Traffic was light.

It was 10:30 in the morning, and cold.

The man's fur-lined collar was turned up, his hands were in his pockets, and he leaned into the wind. Beyond the fence, the road was clean and dry.

The morning sun was buried in clouds. In the dirty light, the man could see the tree a quarter mile ahead.

His pace did not change. His eyes did not leave the tree. The small stones clicked and crunched beneath his shoes.

When he reached the tree he took off his jacket and folded it neatly.

He placed it upon the ground and climbed the tree.

As he moved out onto the limb which extended over the fence, he looked to see that no traffic was approaching. Then he seized the branch with both hands, lowered himself, hung a moment, and dropped onto the highway.

It was a hundred yards wide, the eastbound half of the highway.

He glanced west, saw there was still no traffic coming his way, then began to walk toward the center island. He knew he would never reach it. At this time of day the cars were moving at approximately one hundred sixty miles an hour in the high-acceleration lane. He walked on.

A car passed behind him. He did not look back. If the windows were opaqued, as was usually the case, then the occupants were unaware he had crossed their path. They would hear of it later and examine the front end of their vehicle for possible signs of such an encounter.

A car passed in front of him. Its windows were clear. A glimpse of two faces, their mouths made into O's, was presented to him, then torn from his sight. His own face remained without expression. His pace did not change. Two more cars rushed by, windows darkened. He had crossed perhaps twenty yards of highway.

Twenty-five . . .

Something in the wind, or beneath his feet, told him it was coming. He did not look.

Something in the corner of his eye assured him it was coming. His gait did not alter.

Cecil Green had the windows transpared because he liked it that way. His left hand was inside her blouse and her skirt was piled up on her lap, and his right hand was resting on the lever which would lower the seats. Then she pulled away, making a noise down inside her throat.

His head snapped to the left.

He saw the walking man.

He saw the profile which never turned to face him fully. He saw that the man's gait did not alter.

Then he did not see the man.

There was a slight jar, and the windshield began cleaning itself. Cecil Green raced on.

He opaqued the windows.

"How . . . ?" he asked after she was in his arms again, and sobbing.

"The monitor didn't pick him up. . . ."

"He must not have touched the fence. . . ."

"He must have been out of his mind!"

"Still, he could have picked an easier way."

It could have been any face . . . Mine?

Frightened, Cecil lowered the seats.

* * *

Charles Render was writing the "Necropolis" chapter for *The Missing Link Is Man*, which was to be his first book in over four years. Since his return he had set aside every Tuesday and Thursday afternoon to work on it, isolating himself in his office, filling pages with a chaotic longhand.

"There are many varieties of death, as opposed to dying . . ." he was writing, just as the intercom buzzed briefly, then long, then again briefly.

"Yes?" he asked it, pushing down on the switch.

"You have a visitor," and there was a short intake of breath between "a" and "visitor."

He slipped a small aerosol into his side pocket, then rose and crossed the office.

He opened the door and looked out.

"Doctor . . . Help . . ."

Render took three steps, then dropped to one knee.

"What's the matter?"

"Come—she is . . . sick," he growled.

"Sick? How? What's wrong?"

"Don't know. You come."

Render stared into the unhuman eyes.

"What kind of sick?" he insisted.

"Don't know," repeated the dog. "Won't talk. Sits. I . . . feel, she is sick."

"How did you get here?"

"Drove. Know the co, or, din, ates . . . Left car, outside."

"I'll call her right now." Render turned.

"No good. Won't answer."

He was right.

Render returned to his inner office for his coat and medkit. He glanced out the window and saw where her car was parked, far below, just inside the entrance to the marginal, where the monitor had released it into manual control. If no one assumed that control a car was automatically parked in neutral. The other vehicles were passed around it.

So simple even a dog can drive one, he reflected. *Better get downstairs before a cruiser comes along. It's probably reported itself stopped there already. Maybe not, though. Might still have a few minutes grace.*

He glanced at the huge clock.

"Okay, Sig," he called out. "Let's go."

They took the lift to the ground floor, left by way of the front entrance, and hurried to the car.

Its engine was still idling.

Render opened the passenger-side door and Sigmund leapt in. He squeezed by him into the driver's seat then, but the dog was already pushing the primary coordinates and the address tabs with his paw.

Looks like I'm in the wrong seat.

He lit a cigarette as the car swept ahead into a U-underpass. It emerged on the opposite marginal, sat poised a moment, then joined the traffic flow. The dog directed the car into the high-acceleration lane.

"Oh," said the dog, "oh."

Render felt like patting his head at that moment, but he looked at him, saw that his teeth were bared, and decided against it.

"When did she start acting peculiar?" he asked.

"Came home from work. Did not eat. Would not answer me, when I talked. Just sits."

"Has she ever been like this before?"

"No."

What could have precipitated it?—But maybe she just had a bad day. After all, he's only a dog—sort of. —No. He'd know. But what, then?

"How was she yesterday—and when she left home this morning?"

"Like always."

Render tried calling her again. There was still no answer.

"You, did it," said the dog.

"What do you mean?"

"Eyes. Seeing. You. Machine. Bad."

"No," said Render, and his hand rested on the unit of stun-spray in his pocket.

"Yes," said the dog, turning to him again. "You will, make her well . . ."

"Of course," said Render.

Sigmund stared ahead again.

Render felt physically exhilarated and mentally sluggish. He sought the confusion factor. He had had these feelings about the case since that first session. There was something very unsettling about Eileen Shallot; a combination of high intelligence and helplessness, of determination and vulnerability, of sensitivity and bitterness.

Do I find that especially attractive?—No. It's just the counter-transference, damn it!

"You smell afraid," said the dog.

"Then color me afraid," said Render, "and turn the page."

They slowed for a series of turns, picked up speed again, slowed again, picked up speed again. Finally, they were traveling along a narrow section of roadway through a semi-residential area of town. The car turned up a side street, proceeded about half a mile further, clicked softly beneath its dashboard, and turned into the parking lot behind a high brick apartment building. The click must have been a special servomech which took over from the point where the monitor released it, because the car crawled across the lot, headed into its transparent parking stall, then stopped. Render turned off the ignition.

Sigmund had already opened the door on his side. Render followed him into the building, and they rode the elevator to the fiftieth floor. The dog dashed on ahead up the hallway, pressed his nose against a plate set low in a doorframe, and waited. After a moment, the door swung several inches inward. He pushed it open with his shoulder and entered. Render followed, closing the door behind him.

The apartment was large, its walls pretty much unadorned, its color combinations unnerving. A great library of tapes filled one corner; a monstrous combination-broadcaster stood beside it. There was a wide bowlegged table set in front of the window, and a low couch along the right-hand wall; there was a closed door beside the couch; an archway to the left apparently led to other rooms. Eileen sat in an overstuffed chair in the far corner by the window. Sigmund stood beside the chair.

Render crossed the room and extracted a cigarette from his case. Snapping open his lighter, he held the flame until her head turned in that direction.

"Cigarette?" he asked.

"Charles?"

"Right."

"Yes, thank you. I will."

She held out her hand, accepted the cigarette, put it to her lips.

"Thanks. —What are you doing here?"

"Social call. I happened to be in the neighborhood."

"I didn't hear a buzz, or a knock."

"You must have been dozing. Sig let me in."

"Yes, I must have." She stretched. "What time is it?"

"It's close to four-thirty."

"I've been home over two hours then. . . . Must have been very tired . . ."

"How do you feel now?"

"Fine," she declared. "Care for a cup of coffee?"

"Don't mind if I do."

"A steak to go with it?"

"No, thanks."

"Bacardi in the coffee?"

"Sounds good."

"Excuse me, then. It'll only take a moment."

She went through the door beside the sofa and Render caught a glimpse of a large, shiny, automatic kitchen.

"Well?" he whispered to the dog.

Sigmund shook his head.

"Not same."

Render shook his head.

He deposited his coat on the sofa, folding it carefully about the medkit. He sat beside it and thought.

Did I throw too big a chunk of seeing at once? Is she suffering from depressive side-effects—say, memory repressions, nervous fatigue? Did I upset her sensory adaptation syndrome somehow? Why have I been proceeding so rapidly anyway? There's no real hurry. Am I so damned eager to write the thing up?—Or am I doing it because she wants me to? Could she be that strong, consciously or unconsciously? Or am I that vulnerable—somehow?

She called him to the kitchen to carry out the tray. He set it on the table and seated himself across from her.

"Good coffee," he said, burning his lips on the cup.

"Smart machine," she stated, facing his voice.

Sigmund stretched out on the carpet next to the table, lowered his head between his forepaws, sighed, and closed his eyes.

"I've been wondering," said Render, "whether or not there were any aftereffects to that last session—like increased synesthesiac experiences, or dreams involving forms, or hallucinations or . . ."

"Yes," she said flatly, "dreams."

"What kind?"

"That last session. I've dreamt it over, and over."

"Beginning to end?"

"No, there's no special order to the events. We're riding through the city, or over the bridge, or sitting at the table, or walking toward the car—just flashes, like that. Vivid ones."

"What sort of feelings accompany these—flashes?"

"I don't know. They're all mixed up."

"What are your feelings now, as you recall them?"

"The same, all mixed up."

"Are you afraid?"

"N-no. I don't think so."

"Do you want to take a vacation from the thing? Do you feel we've been proceeding too rapidly?"

"No. That's not it at all. It's—well, it's like learning to swim. When you finally learn how, why then you swim and you swim and you swim until you're all exhausted. Then you just lie there gasping in air and remembering what it was like, while your friends all hover and chew you out for overexerting yourself—and it's a good feeling, even though you do take a chill and there's pins and needles inside all your muscles. At least, that's the way I do things. I felt that way after the first session and after this last one. First times are always very special times. . . . The pins and the needles are gone though, and I've caught my breath again. Lord, I don't want to stop now! I feel fine."

"Do you usually take a nap in the afternoon?"

The ten red nails of her fingers moved across the tabletop as she stretched.

". . . Tired," she smiled, swallowing a yawn. "Half the staff's on vacation or sick leave and I've been beating my brains out all week. I was about ready to fall on my face when I left work. I feel all right now that I've rested, though."

She picked up her coffee cup with both hands, took a large swallow.

"Uh-huh," he said. "Good. I was a bit worried about you. I'm glad to see there was no reason."

She laughed.

"Worried? You've read Doctor Riscomb's notes on my analysis—and on the ONT&R trial—and you think I'm the sort to worry about? Ha! I have an operationally beneficent neurosis concerning my adequacy as a human being. It focuses my energies, coordinates my efforts toward achievement. It enhances my sense of identity. . . ."

"You do have one hell of a memory," he noted. "That's almost verbatim."

"Of course."

"You had Sigmund worried today, too."

"Sig? How?"

The dog stirred uneasily, opened one eye.

"Yes," he growled, glaring up at Render. "He needs, a ride, home."

"Have you been driving the car again?"

"Yes."

"After I told you not to?"

"Yes."

"Why?"

"I was a, fraid. You would, not, answer me, when I talked."

"I was *very* tired—and if you ever take the car again, I'm going to have the door fixed so you can't come and go as you please."

"Sorry."

"There's nothing wrong with me."

"I, see."

"You are *never* to do it again."

"Sorry." His eye never left Render; it was like a burning lens.

Render looked away.

"Don't be too hard on the poor fellow," he said. "After all, he thought you were ill and he went for the doctor. Supposing he'd been right? You'd owe him thanks, not a scolding."

Unmollified, Sigmund glared a moment longer and closed his eye.

"He has to be told when he does wrong," she finished.

"I suppose," he said, drinking his coffee. "No harm done, anyhow. Since I'm here, let's talk shop. I'm writing something and I'd like an opinion."

"Great. Give me a footnote?"

"Two or three. —In your opinion, do the general underlying motivations that lead to suicide differ in different periods of history or in different cultures?"

"My well-considered opinion is no, they don't," she said. "Frustrations can lead to depressions or frenzies;

and if these are severe enough, they can lead to self-destruction. You ask me about motivations and I think they stay pretty much the same. I feel this is a cross-cultural, cross-temporal aspect of the human condition. I don't think it could be changed without changing the basic nature of man."

"Okay. Check. Now, what of the inciting element?" he asked. "Let man be a constant, his environment is still a variable. If he is placed in an overprotective life-situation, do you feel it would take more or less to depress him—or stimulate him to frenzy—than it would take in a not so protective environment?"

"Hm. Being case-oriented, I'd say it would depend on the man. But I see what you're driving at: a mass predisposition to jump out windows at the drop of a hat—the window even opening itself for you, because you asked it to—the revolt of the bored masses. I don't like the notion. I hope it's wrong."

"So do I, but I was thinking of symbolic suicides too—functional disorders that occur for pretty flimsy reasons."

"Aha! Your lecture last month: autopsychomimesis. I have the tape. Well-told, but I can't agree."

"Neither can I, now. I'm rewriting that whole section —'Thanatos in Cloudcuckooland,' I'm calling it. It's really the death-instinct moved nearer the surface."

"If I get you a scalpel and a cadaver, will you cut out the death-instinct and let me touch it?"

"Couldn't," he put the grin into his voice, "it would be all used up in a cadaver. Find me a volunteer though, and he'll prove my case by volunteering."

"Your logic is unassailable," she smiled. "Get us some more coffee, okay?"

Render went to the kitchen, spiked and filled the cups, drank a glass of water, returned to the living room. Eileen had not moved; neither had Sigmund.

"What do you do when you're not busy being a Shaper?" she asked him.

"The same things most people do—eat, drink, sleep, talk, visit friends and not-friends, visit places, read . . ."

"Are you a forgiving man?"

"Sometimes. Why?"

"Then forgive me. I argued with a woman today, a woman named DeVille."

"What about?"

"You—and she accused me of such things it were better my mother had not borne me. Are you going to marry her?"

"No, marriage is like alchemy. It served an important purpose once, but I hardly feel it's here to stay."

"Good."

"What did you say to her?"

"I gave her a clinic referral card that said, 'Diagnosis: Bitch. Prescription: Drug therapy and a tight gag.'"

"Oh," said Render, showing interest.

"She tore it up and threw it in my face."

"I wonder why?"

She shrugged, smiled, made a gridwork on the tablecloth.

"'Fathers and elders, I ponder,'" sighed Render, "'what is hell?'"

"'I maintain it is the suffering of being unable to love,'" she finished. "Was Dostoevsky right?"

"I doubt it. I'd put him into group therapy, myself. That'd be *real* hell for him—with all those people acting like his characters and enjoying it so."

Render put down his cup and pushed his chair away from the table.

"I suppose you must be going now?"

"I really should," said Render.

"And I can't interest you in food?"

"No."

She stood.

"Okay, I'll get my coat."

"I could drive back myself and just set the car to return."

"No! I'm frightened by the notion of empty cars driving around the city. I'd feel the thing was haunted for the next two-and-a-half weeks.

"Besides," she said, passing through the archway, "you promised me Winchester Cathedral."

"You want to do it today?"

"If you can be persuaded."

As Render stood deciding, Sigmund rose to his feet. He stood directly before him and stared upward into his eyes. He opened his mouth and closed it, several times, but no sounds emerged. Then he turned away and left the room.

"No," Eileen's voice came back, "you will stay here until I return."

Render picked up his coat and put it on, stuffing the medkit into the far pocket.

As they walked up the hall toward the elevator, Render thought he heard a very faint and very distant howling sound.

In this place, of all places, Render knew he was the master of all things.

He was at home on those alien worlds, without time, those worlds where flowers copulate and the stars do battle in the heavens, falling at last to the ground, bleeding, like so many split and shattered chalices, and the seas part to reveal stairways leading down, and arms emerge from caverns, waving torches that flame like liquid faces—a midwinter night's nightmare, summer go a-begging, Render knew—for he had visited those worlds on a professional basis for the better part of a decade. With the crooking of a finger he could isolate the sorcerers, bring them to trial for treason against the realm—aye, and he could execute them, could appoint their successors.

Fortunately, this trip was only a courtesy call . . .

He moved forward through the glade, seeking her.

He could feel her awakening presence all about him.

He pushed through the branches, stood beside the lake. It was cold, blue, and bottomless, the lake, reflecting that slender willow which had become the station of her arrival.

"Eileen!"

The willow swayed toward him, swayed away.

"Eileen! Come forth!"

Leaves fell, floated upon the lake, disturbed its mirror-like placidity, distorted the reflections.

"Eileen?"

All the leaves yellowed at once then, dropped down into the water. The tree ceased its swaying. There was a strange sound in the darkening sky, like the humming of high wires on a cold day.

Suddenly there was a double file of moons passing through the heavens.

Render selected one, reached up, and pressed it. The others vanished as he did so, and the world brightened; the humming went out of the air.

He circled the lake to gain a subjective respite from the rejection-action and his counter to it. He moved up along an aisle of pines toward the place where he wanted the cathedral to occur. Birds sang now in the trees. The wind came softly by him. He felt her presence quite strongly.

"Here, Eileen. Here."

She walked beside him then, green silk, hair of bronze, eyes of molten emerald; she wore an emerald in her forehead. She walked in green slippers over the pine needles, saying: "What happened?"

"You were afraid."

"Why?"

"Perhaps you fear the cathedral. Are you a witch?" he smiled.

"Yes, but it's my day off."

He laughed, and he took her arm, and they rounded an island of foliage, and there was the cathedral reconstructed on a grassy rise, pushing its way above them and above the trees, climbing into the middle air, breathing out organ notes, reflecting a stray ray of sunlight from a pane of glass.

"Hold tight to the world," he said. "Here comes the guided tour."

They moved forward and entered.

"'. . . With its floor-to-ceiling shafts, like so many huge tree trunks, it achieves a ruthless control over its spaces,'" he said. "—Got that from the guidebook. This is the north transept. . . .'"

"'Greensleeves,'" she said, "the organ is playing 'Greensleeves.'"

"So it is. You can't blame me for that though.—Observe the scalloped capitals—"

"I want to go nearer to the music."

"Very well. This way then."

Render felt that something was wrong. He could not put his finger on it.

Everything retained its solidity. . . .

Something passed rapidly then, high above the cathedral, uttering a sonic boom. Render smiled at that, remembering now; it was like a slip of the tongue: for a moment he had confused Eileen with Jill—yes, that was what had happened.

Why, then . . .

A burst of white was the altar. He had never seen it before, anywhere. All the walls were dark and cold about them. Candles flickered in corners and high niches. The organ chorded thunder under invisible hands.

Render knew that something was wrong.

He turned to Eileen Shallot, whose hat was a green cone towering up into the darkness, trailing wisps of green veiling. Her throat was in shadow, but . . .

"That necklace—Where?"

"I don't know," she smiled.

The goblet she held radiated a rosy light. It was reflected from her emerald. It washed him like a draft of cool air.

"Drink?" she asked.

"Stand still," he ordered.

He willed the walls to fall down. They swam in shadow.

"Stand still!" he repeated urgently. "Don't do anything. Try not even to think.

"—Fall down!" he cried. And the walls were blasted in all directions and the roof was flung over the top of the world, and they stood amid ruins lighted by a single taper. The night was black as pitch.

"Why did you do that?" she asked, still holding the goblet out toward him.

"Don't think. Don't think anything," he said. "Relax. You are very tired. As that candle flickers and wanes so does your consciousness. You can barely keep awake. You can hardly stay on your feet. Your eyes are closing. There is nothing to see here anyway."

He willed the candle to go out. It continued to burn.

"I'm not tired. Please have a drink."

He heard organ music through the night. A different tune, one he did not recognize at first.

"I need your cooperation."

"All right. Anything."

"Look! The moon!" he pointed.

She looked upward and the moon appeared from behind an inky cloud.

". . . And another, and another."

Moons, like strung pearls, proceeded across the blackness.

"The last one will be red," he stated.

It was.

He reached out then with his right index finger, slid his arm sideways along his field of vision, then tried to touch the red moon.

His arm ached, it burned. He could not move it.

"Wake up!" he screamed.

The red moon vanished, and the white ones.

"Please take a drink."

He dashed the goblet from her hand and turned away. When he turned back she was still holding it before him.

"A drink?"

He turned and fled into the night.

It was like running through a waist-high snowdrift. It was wrong. He was compounding the error by running —he was minimizing his strength, maximizing hers. It was sapping his energies, draining him.

He stood still in the midst of the blackness.

"The world around me moves," he said. "I am its center."

"Please have a drink," she said, and he was standing in the glade beside their table set beside the lake. The lake was black and the moon was silver, and high, and out of his reach. A single candle flickered on the table, making her hair as silver as her dress. She wore the moon on her brow. A bottle of Romanée-Conti stood on the white cloth beside a wide-brimmed wine glass. It was filled to overflowing, that glass, and rosy beads clung to its lip. He was very thirsty, and she was lovelier than anyone he had ever seen before, and her necklace sparkled, and the breeze came cool off the lake, and there was something—something he should remember . . .

He took a step toward her and his armor clinked lightly as he moved. He reached toward the glass and his right arm stiffened with pain and fell back to his side.

"You are wounded!"

Slowly, he turned his head. The blood flowed from the open wound in his bicep and ran down his arm and dripped from his fingertips. His armor had been breached. He forced himself to look away.

"Drink this, love. It will heal you."

She stood.

"I will hold the glass."

He stared at her as she raised it to his lips.

"Who am I?" he asked.

She did not answer him, but something replied— within a splashing of waters out over the lake:

"You are Render, the Shaper."

"Yes, I remember," he said; and turning his mind to

the one lie which might break the entire illusion he forced his mouth to say: "Eileen Shallot, I hate you."

The world shuddered and swam about him, was shaken, as by a huge sob.

"Charles!" she screamed, and the blackness swept over them.

"Wake up! Wake up!" he cried, and his right arm burned and ached and bled in the darkness.

He stood alone in the midst of a white plain. It was silent, it was endless. It sloped away toward the edges of the world. It gave off its own light, and the sky was no sky, but was nothing overhead. Nothing. He was alone. His own voice echoed back to him from the end of the world: ". . . hate you," it said, ". . . hate you."

He dropped to his knees. He was Render.

He wanted to cry.

A red moon appeared above the plain, casting a ghastly light over the entire expanse. There was a wall of mountains to the left of him, another to his right.

He raised his right arm. He helped it with his left hand. He clutched his wrist, extended his index finger. He reached for the moon.

Then there came a howl from high in the mountains, a great wailing cry—half-human, all challenge, all loneliness, and all remorse. He saw it then, treading upon the mountains, its tail brushing the snow from their highest peaks, the ultimate loup-garou of the North—Fenris, son of Loki—raging at the heavens.

It leapt into the air. It swallowed the moon.

It landed near him, and its great eyes blazed yellow. It stalked him on soundless pads, across the cold white fields that lay between the mountains; and he backed away from it, up hills and down slopes, over crevasses and rifts, through valleys, past stalagmites and pinnacles—under the edges of glaciers, beside frozen river beds, and always downwards—until its hot breath bathed him and its laughing mouth was opened above him.

He turned then and his feet became two gleaming rivers carrying him away.

The world jumped backwards. He glided over the slopes. Downward. Speeding—

Away . . .

He looked back over his shoulder.

In the distance, the gray shape loped after him.

He felt that it could narrow the gap if it chose. He had to move faster.

The world reeled about him. Snow began to fall.

He raced on.

Ahead, a blur, a broken outline.

He tore through the veils of snow which now seemed to be falling upward from off the ground—like strings of bubbles.

He approached the shattered form.

Like a swimmer he approached—unable to open his mouth to speak, for fear of drowning—of drowning and not knowing, of never knowing.

He could not check his forward motion; he was swept tidelike toward the wreck. He came to a stop, at last, before it.

Some things never change. They are things which have long ceased to exist as objects and stand solely as never-to-be-calendared occasions outside that sequence of elements called Time.

Render stood there and did not care if Fenris leapt upon his back and ate his brains. He had covered his eyes, but he could not stop the seeing. Not this time. He did not care about anything. Most of himself lay dead at his feet.

There was a howl. A gray shape swept past him.

The baleful eyes and bloody muzzle rooted within the wrecked car, champing through the steel, the glass, groping inside for . . .

"No! Brute! Chewer of corpses!" he cried. "The dead are sacred! *My* dead are sacred!"

He had a scalpel in his hand then, and he slashed expertly at the tendons, the bunches of muscle on the

straining shoulders, the soft belly, the ropes of the
arteries.

Weeping, he dismembered the monster, limb by limb,
and it bled and it bled, fouling the vehicle and the
remains within it with its infernal animal juices, dripping and running until the whole plain was reddened
and writhing about them.

Render fell across the pulverized hood, and it was soft
and warm and dry. He wept upon it.

"Don't cry," she said.

He was hanging onto her shoulder then, holding her
tightly, there beside the black lake beneath the moon
that was Wedgwood. A single candle flickered upon
their table. She held the glass to his lips.

"Please drink it."

"Yes, give it to me!"

He gulped the wine that was all softness and light-
ness. It burned within him. He felt his strength returning.

"I am . . ."

"—Render, the Shaper," splashed the lake.

"No!"

He turned and ran again, looking for the wreck. He
had to go back, to return . . .

"You can't."

"I can!" he cried. "I can, if I try. . . ."

Yellow flames coiled through the thick air. Yellow
serpents. They coiled, glowing, about his ankles. Then
through the murk, two-headed and towering, approached his Adversary.

Small stones rattled past him. An overpowering odor
corkscrewed up his nose and into his head.

"Shaper!" came the bellow from one head.

"You have returned for the reckoning!" called the
other.

Render stared, remembering.

"No reckoning, Thaumiel," he said. "I beat you and I
chained you for—Rothman, yes, it was Rothman—the

cabalist." He traced a pentagram in the air. "Return to Qliphoth. I banish you."

"This place be Qliphoth."

". . . By Khamael, the angel of blood, by the hosts of Seraphim, in the Name of Elohim Gebor, I bid you vanish!"

"Not this time," laughed both heads.

It advanced.

Render backed slowly away, his feet bound by the yellow serpents. He could feel the chasm opening behind him. The world was a jigsaw puzzle coming apart. He could see the pieces separating.

"Vanish!"

The giant roared out its double-laugh.

Render stumbled.

"This way, love!"

She stood within a small cave to his right.

He shook his head and backed toward the chasm.

Thaumiel reached out toward him.

Render toppled back over the edge.

"Charles!" she screamed, and the world shook itself apart with her wailing.

"Then Vernichtung," he answered as he fell. "I join you in darkness."

Everything came to an end.

"I want to see Doctor Charles Render."

"I'm sorry, that is impossible."

"But I skip-jetted all the way here, just to thank him. I'm a new man! He changed my life!"

"I'm sorry, Mister Erikson. When you called this morning, I told you it was impossible."

"Sir, I'm Representative Erikson—and Render once did me a great service."

"Then you can do him one now. Go home."

"You can't talk to me that way!"

"I just did. Please leave. Maybe next year sometime . . ."

"But a few words can do wonders. . . ."

"Save them!"

"I-I'm sorry . . ."

Lovely as it was, pinked over with the morning—the slopping, steaming bowl of the sea—he knew that it *had* to end. Therefore . . .

He descended the high tower stairway and he entered the courtyard. He crossed to the bower of roses and he looked down upon the pallet set in its midst.

"Good morrow, m'lord," he said.

"To you the same," said the knight, his blood mingling with the earth, the flowers, the grasses, flowing from his wound, sparkling over his armor, dripping from his fingertips.

"Naught hath healed?"

The knight shook his head.

"I empty. I wait."

"Your waiting is near ended."

"What mean you?" He sat upright.

"The ship. It approacheth harbor."

The knight stood. He leaned his back against a mossy tree trunk. He stared at the huge, bearded servitor who continued to speak, words harsh with barbaric accents:

"It cometh like a dark swan before the wind—returning."

"Dark, you say? Dark?"

"The sails be black, Lord Tristram."

"You lie!"

"Do you wish to see? To see for yourself?—Look then!"

He gestured.

The earth quaked, the wall toppled. The dust swirled and settled. From where they stood they could see the ship moving into the harbor on the wings of the night.

"No! You lied!—See! They are white!"

The dawn danced upon the waters. The shadows fled from the ship's sails.

"No, you fool! Black! They *must* be!"

"White! White!—Isolde! You have kept faith! You have returned!"

He began running toward the harbor.

"Come back!—Your wound! You are ill—Stop . . ."

The sails were white beneath a sun that was a red button which the servitor reached quickly to touch.

Night fell.

After dinner Janet and I both went over to Christine's house to see the proofs. While I studied the pictures, Christine and Janet went back to the kitchen to talk and make coffee. I finished and leaned back in my chair waiting for their return. Without any perceptible difference in my thoughts, my position, anything, I was seeing Janet through Christine's eyes. Janet looked shocked and unbelieving.

I stared at her and began to see other faces there, too. Younger, clearer eyes, and smoother-skinned, emptier-looking. I turned my head abruptly as something else started to emerge. I knew that if I had tried, I would have seen all the personality traits, including the ugliness, the pettiness, everything there was that went into her.

"What is it?" Janet asked, alarm in her voice.

I shook my head, *Christine's* head. She tried to speak and I wouldn't let her. Without any warning I had crossed the threshold of belief. I knew I could enter her, could use her, could examine whatever was in her mind without her being able to do anything about it. I knew in that same flash that she didn't realize what was happening, that she felt haunted, or crazy, but that she had no idea that another personality was inside her. I pulled away so suddenly that I almost let her fall down.

From the other room I heard Janet's cry, followed by the sound of breaking glass. I hurried to the kitchen to find her standing over Christine, who was sitting on a stool looking dazed and bewildered and very frightened.

"What's wrong?" I asked,

Janet shook her head. "I dropped a glass," she said, daring me not to believe.

THE TOR DOUBLE NOVELS

A Meeting with Medusa by Arthur C. Clarke/*Green Mars* by Kim Stanley Robinson

Hardfought by Greg Bear/*Cascade Point* by Timothy Zahn

Born with the Dead by Robert Silverberg/*The Saliva Tree* by Brian W. Aldiss

No Truce with Kings by Poul Anderson/*Ship of Shadows* by Fritz Leiber

Enemy Mine by Barry B. Longyear/*Another Orphan* by John Kessel

Screwtop by Vonda N. McIntyre/*The Girl Who Was Plugged In* by James Tiptree, Jr.

The Nemesis from Terra by Leigh Brackett/*Battle for the Stars* by Edmond Hamilton

The Ugly Little Boy by Isaac Asimov/*The [Widget], The [Wadget], and Boff* by Theodore Sturgeon

Sailing to Byzantium by Robert Silverberg/*Seven American Nights* by Gene Wolfe

Houston, Houston, Do You Read? by James Tiptree, Jr./*Souls* by Joanna Russ

*The Blind Geometer by Kim Stanley Robinson/*The New Atlantis* by Ursula K. Le Guin

*forthcoming

KATE WILHELM
THE
INFINITY
BOX

A TOM DOHERTY ASSOCIATES BOOK
NEW YORK

This is a work of fiction. All the characters and events portrayed in this book are fictitious, and any resemblance to real people or events is purely coincidental.

THE INFINITY BOX

Copyright © 1971 by Damon Knight for *Orbit 9;* copyright © 1975 by Kate Wilhelm

All rights reserved, including the right to reproduce this book or portions thereof in any form.

A TOR Book
Published by Tom Doherty Associates, Inc.
49 West 24 Street
New York, NY 10010

Cover art by Royo

ISBN: 0-812-55879-0   Can. ISBN: 0-812-50266-3

First edition: September 1989

Printed in the United States of America

0 9 8 7 6 5 4 3 2 1

It was a bad day from beginning to end. Late in the afternoon, just when I was ready to light the fuse to blow up the lab, with Lenny in it, Janet called from the hospital.

"Honey, it's the little Bronson boy. We can't do anything with him, and he has his mother and father in a panic. He's sure that we're trying to electrocute him, and they half believe it. They're demanding that we take the cast off and remove the suit."

Lenny sat watching my face. He began to move things out of reach: the glass of pencils, coffee mugs, ashtray. . . .

"Can't Groppi do anything?" He was the staff psychologist.

"Not this time. He doesn't really understand the suit either. I think he's afraid of it. Can you come over here and talk to them?"

"Sure. Sure. We just blew up about five thousand dollars' worth of equipment with a faulty transformer. Lenny's quitting again. Some son of a bitch mislaid our order for wafer resisters. . . . I'll be over in half an hour."

"What?" Lenny asked. He looked like a dope, thick build, the biggest pair of hands you'd ever see outside a football field, shoulders that didn't need padding to look padded. Probably he was one of the best electronics men in the world. He was forty-six, and had brought up three sons alone. He never mentioned their mother and I didn't know if she was dead, or just gone. He was

my partner in the firm of Laslow and Leonard Electronics.

"The Bronson kid's scared to death of the suit we put on him yesterday. First time they turned it on, he panicked. I'll run over and see. Where's that sleeve?" I rummaged futilely and Lenny moved stolidly toward a cabinet and pulled out the muslin sleeve and small control box. Once in a while he'd smile, but that was the only emotion that I'd ever seen on his face, a quiet smile, usually when something worked against the odds, or when his sons did something exceptionally nice— like get a full paid scholarship to MIT, or Harvard, as the third one had done that fall.

"Go on home after you see the kid," Lenny said. "I'll clean up in here and try to run down the wafers."

"Okay. See you tomorrow."

Children's Hospital was fifteen miles away, traffic was light at that time of day, and I made it under the half hour I'd promised. Janet met me in the downstairs foyer.

"Eddie, did you bring the sleeve? I thought maybe if you let Mr. Bronson feel it . . ."

I held it up and she grinned. Janet, suntanned, with red, sunstreaked hair, freckles, and lean to the point of thinness, was my idea of a beautiful woman. We had been married for twelve years.

"Where are the parents?"

"In Dr. Reisman's office. They were just upsetting Mike more than he was already."

"Okay, first Mike. Come on."

Mike Bronson was eight. Three months ago, the first day of school vacation, he had been run over and killed by a diesel truck. He had been listed DOA; someone had detected an echo of life, but they said he couldn't survive the night. They operated, and gave him a week, then a month, and six weeks ago they had done more surgery and said probably he'd make it. Crushed spine, crushed pelvis, multiple fractures in both legs. One of the problems was that the boy was eight, and growing.

His hormonal system didn't seem to get the message that he was critically injured, and that things should stop for a year or so, and that meant that his body cast had to be changed frequently and it meant that while his bones grew together again, and lengthened, his muscles would slowly atrophy, and when he was removed from the cast finally, there'd be a bundle of bones held together by pale skin and not much else.

At Mike's door I motioned for Janet to stay outside. One more white uniform, I thought, he didn't need right now. They had him in a private room, temporarily, I assumed, because of his reaction to the suit. He couldn't move his head, but he heard me come in, and when I got near enough so he could see me, his eyes were wide with fear. He was a good-looking boy with big brown eyes that knew too much of pain and fear.

"You a cub scout?" I asked.

He could talk some, a throaty whisper, when he wanted to. He didn't seem to want to then. I waited a second or two, then said, "You know what a ham radio set is, I suppose. If you could learn the Morse code, I could fix a wire so that you could use the key." I was looking around his bed, as if to see if it could be done, talking to myself. "Put a screen with the code up there, where you could see it. Sort of a learning machine. Work the wire with your tongue at first, until they uncover your hands anyway. Course not everybody wants to talk to Australia or Russia or Brazil or ships at sea. All done with wires, some people are afraid of wires and things like that."

He was watching me intently now, his eyes following my gaze as I studied the space above his head. He was ready to deal in five minutes. "You stop bitching about the suit, and I start on the ham set. Right?" His eyes sparkled at that kind of language and he whispered, "Right."

"Now the parents," I told Janet in the hall. "He's okay."

Bronson was apelike, with great muscular, hairy

forearms. I never did say who I was, or why I was there, anything at all. "Hold out your arm," I ordered. He looked from me to Dr. Reisman, who was in a sweat by then. The doctor nodded. I put the sleeve on his arm, then put an inflatable splint on it, inflating it slightly more than was necessary, but I was mad. "Move your fingers," I ordered. He tried. I attached the jack to the sleeve wire and plugged it in, and then I played his arm and hand muscles like a piano. He gaped. "That's what we're doing to your son. If we don't do it, when he comes out of that cast he'll be like a stick doll. His muscles will waste away to nothing. He'll weight twenty-five pounds, maybe." That was a guess, but it made the point. "Every time they change the cast, we change the program, so that every muscle in his body will be stimulated under computer control, slightly at first, then stronger and stronger as he gets better." I started to undo the splint. The air came out with a teakettle hiss. "You wouldn't dream of telling Dr. Thorne how to operate on your boy. Don't tell me my business, unless you know it better than I do."

"But . . . Did it hurt?" Mrs. Bronson asked.

"No," Bronson said, flexing his fingers. "It just tingled a little bit. Felt sort of good."

I removed the sleeve and folded it carefully, and at the door I heard Mrs. Bronson's whisper, "Who is he?" and Janet's haughty answer, "That's Edward Laslow, the inventor of the Laslow Suit."

Enrico Groppi met me in the corridor. "I just came from Mike's room. Thanks. Want a drink?" Groppi was an eclectic—he took from here, there, anything that worked he was willing to incorporate into his system.

"That's an idea." I followed him to his office, left word for Janet to meet me there, and tried not to think about the possibility that the suit wouldn't work, that I'd built up false hopes, that Mike would come to hate me and everything I symbolized. . . .

I drove Janet home, leaving her car in the hospital lot overnight. That meant that I'd have to drive her to work

in the morning, but it seemed too silly to play follow the leader back the county roads. To get home we took the interstate highway first, then a four-lane state road, then a two-lane county road, then a right turn off onto a dirt road, and that was ours. Sweet Brier Lane. Five one-acre lots, with woods all around, and a hill behind us, and a brook. If any of us prayed at all, it was only that the county engineers wouldn't discover the existence of Sweet Brier Lane and come in with their bulldozers and road-building equipment and turn us into a real development.

Our house was the third one on the narrow road. First on the left was Bill Glaser, a contractor, nice fellow if you didn't have to do more than wave and say hi from time to time. Then on the right came the Donlevy house that had been empty for almost three years while Peter Donlevy was engaged in an exchange program with teachers from England. He was at Cambridge, and from the Christmas cards that we got from them, they might never return. Then, again on the right, our house, set far back behind oak trees that made grass-growing almost impossible. Farther down and across the lane was Earl Klinger's house. He was with the math department of the university. And finally the lane dead-ended at the driveway of Lucas Malek and his wife. He was in his sixties, retired from the insurance business, and to be avoided if possible. An immigrant from East Europe, Hungary or some place like that, he was bored and talked endlessly if encouraged. We were on polite, speaking terms with everyone on the lane, but the Donlevys had been our friends; with them gone, we had drawn inward, and had very little to do with the neighbors. We could have borrowed sugar from any of them, or got a lift to town, or counted on them to call the fire department if our house started to burn down, but there was no close camaraderie there.

It was our fault. If we had wanted friends we certainly could have found them in that small group of talented and intelligent people. But we were busy. Janet with her

work at the hospital where she was a physical therapist, and I at my laboratory that was just now after fourteen years starting to show a bit of profit. It could have got out of the red earlier, but Lenny and I both believed in updating the equipment whenever possible, so it had taken time.

It was a warm day, early in September, without a hint yet that summer had had it. I had the windows open, making talk impossible. Janet and I could talk or not. There were still times when we stayed up until morning, just talking, and then again weeks went by with nothing more than the sort of thing that has to take place between husband and wife. No strain either way, nothing but ease lay between us. We had a good thing, and we knew it.

We were both startled, and a little upset, when we saw a moving van and a dilapidated station wagon in the driveway of the Donlevy house.

"They wouldn't come back without letting us know," Janet said.

"Not a chance. Maybe they sold it."

"But without a sign, or any real-estate people coming around?"

"They could have been here day after day without our knowing."

"But not without Ruth Klinger knowing about it. She would have told us."

I drove past the house slowly, craning to see something that would give a hint. Only the station wagon, with a Connecticut plate. It was an eight-year-old model, in need of a paint job. It didn't look too hopeful.

Every afternoon a woman from a nearby subdivision came to stay with the children and to straighten up generally until we got home. Mrs. Durrell was as mystified as we about the van and the newcomer.

"Haven't seen a sign of anyone poking about over there. Rusty says that they're just moving boxes in, heavy boxes." Rusty, eleven, probably knew exactly how many boxes, and their approximate weight. "The kids

are down at the brook watching them unload," Mrs. Durrell went on. "They're hoping for more kids, I guess. Rusty keeps coming up to report, and so far, only one woman, and a lot of boxes." She talked herself out of the kitchen, across the terrace, and down the drive to her car, her voice fading out gradually.

Neither Pete Donlevy nor I had any inclination for gardening, and our yards, separated by the brook, were heavily wooded, so that his house was not visible from ours, but down at the brook there was a clear view between the trees. While Janet changed into shorts and sandals, I wandered down to have a look along with Rusty and Laura. They were both Janet's kids. Redheads, with freckles, and vivid blue-green eyes, skinny arms and legs; sometimes I found myself studying one or the other of them intently for a hint of my genes there, without success. Laura was eight. I spotted her first, sitting on the bridge made of two fallen trees. We had lopped the branches off and the root mass and just left them there. Pete Donlevy and I had worked three weekends on those trees, cutting up the branches for our fireplaces, rolling the two trunks close together to make a footbridge. We had consumed approximately ten gallons of beer during those weekends.

"Hi, Dad," Rusty called from above me. I located him high on the right-angled branch of an oak tree. "We have a new neighbor."

I nodded and sat down next to Laura. "Any kids?"

"No. Just a lady so far."

"Young? Old? Fat?"

"Tiny. I don't know if young or old, can't tell. She runs around like young."

"With lots of books," Rusty said from his better vantage point.

"No furniture?"

"Nope. Just suitcases and a trunk full of clothes, and boxes of books. And cameras, and tripods."

"And a black-and-white dog," Laura added.

I tossed bits of bark into the brook and watched them

bob and whirl their way downstream. Presently we went back to the house, and later we grilled hamburgers on the terrace, and had watermelon for dessert. I didn't get a glimpse of the tiny lady.

Sometime during the night I was brought straight up in bed by a wail that was animal-like, thin, high-pitched, inhuman. "Laura!"

Janet was already out of bed; in the pale light from the hall, she was a flash of white gown darting out the doorway. The wail was repeated, and by then I was on my way to Laura's room too. She was standing in the middle of the floor, her short pajamas white, her eyes wide open, showing mostly white also. Her hands were partially extended before her, fingers widespread, stiff.

"Laura!" Janet said. It was a command, low-voiced, but imperative. The child didn't move. I put my arm about her shoulders, not wanting to frighten her more than she was by the nightmare. She was rigid and unmoving, as stiff as a catatonic.

"Pull back the sheet," I told Janet. "I'll carry her back to bed." It was like lifting a wooden dummy. No response, no flexibility, no life. My skin crawled, and fear made a sour taste in my mouth. Back in her bed, Laura suddenly sighed, and her eyelids fluttered once or twice, then closed and she was in a normal sleep. I lifted her hand, her wrist was limp, her fingers dangled loosely.

Janet stayed with her for a few minutes, but she didn't wake up, and finally Janet joined me in the kitchen, where I had poured a glass of milk and was sipping it.

"I never saw anything like that," Janet said. She was pale, and shaking.

"A nightmare, honey. Too much watermelon, or something. More than likely she won't remember anything about it. Just as well."

We didn't discuss it. There wasn't anything to say. Who knows anything about nightmares? But I had trouble getting back to sleep again, and when I did, I

dreamed off and on the rest of the night, waking up time after time with the memory of a dream real enough to distort my thinking so that I couldn't know if I was sleeping in bed, or floating somewhere else and dreaming of the bed.

Laura didn't remember any of the dream, but she was fascinated, and wanted to talk about it: what had she been doing when we found her? how had she sounded when she shrieked? and so on. After about five minutes it got to be a bore and I refused to say another word. Mornings were always bad anyway; usually I was the last to leave the house, but that morning I had to drive Janet to work, so we all left at the same time, the kids to catch the schoolbus at the end of the lane, Janet to go to the hospital, and me to go to the lab eventually. At the end of the lane when I stopped to let the kids hop out, we saw our new neighbor. She was walking a Dalmatian, and she smiled and nodded. But Laura surprised us all by calling out to her, greeting her like a real friend. When I drove away I could see them standing there, the dog sniffing the kids interestedly, the woman and Laura talking.

"Well," was all I could think to say. Laura usually was the shy one, the last to make friends with people, the last to speak to company, the first to break away from a group of strangers.

"She seems all right," Janet said.

"Let's introduce ourselves tonight. Maybe she's someone from around here, someone from school." And I wondered where else Laura could have met her without our meeting her also.

We didn't meet her that day.

I got tied up, and it was after eight when I got home, tired and disgusted by a series of mishaps again at the lab. Janet didn't help by saying that maybe we had too many things going at once for just the two of us to keep track of. Knowing she was right didn't make the comment any easier to take. Lenny and I were jealous of our

shop and lab. We didn't want to bring in an outsider, and secretly I knew that I didn't want to be bothered with the kind of bookkeeping that would be involved.

"You can't have it both ways," Janet said. Sometimes she didn't know when to drop it. "Either you remain at the level you were at a couple of years ago, patenting little things every so often, and leave the big jobs to the companies that have the manpower, or else you let your staff grow along with your ideas."

I ate warmed-over roast beef without tasting it, and drank two gin-and-tonics. The television sound was bad and that annoyed me, even though it was three rooms away with the doors between closed.

"Did you get started on Mike's ham set yet?" Janet asked, clearing the table.

"Christ!" I had forgotten. I took my coffee and headed for the basement. "I'll get at it. I've got what I need. Don't wait up. If I don't do it tonight, I won't get to it for days." I had suits being tested at three different hospitals, Mike's, one at a geriatric clinic where an eighty-year-old man was recovering from a broken hip, and one in a veterans' hospital where a young man in a coma was guinea pig. I was certain the suit would be more effective than the daily massage that such patients usually received, when there was sufficient help to administer such massage to begin with. The suits were experimental and needed constant checking, the programs needed constant supervision for this first application. And it was my baby. So I worked that night on the slides for Mike Bronson, and it was nearly two when I returned to the kitchen, keyed up and tense from too much coffee and too many cigarettes.

I wandered outside and walked for several minutes back through the woods, ending up at the bridge, staring at the Donlevy house where there was a light on in Pete Donlevy's study. I wondered again about the little woman who had moved in, wondered if others had joined her, or if they would join her. It didn't seem practical for one woman to rent such a big house. I was

leaning against the same tree that Rusty had perched in watching the unloading of boxes. I wasn't thinking of anything in particular, images were flitting through my mind, snaps, scraps of talk, bits and pieces of unfinished projects, disconnected words. I must have closed my eyes. It was dark under the giant oak and there was nothing to see anyway, except the light in Pete's study, and that was only a small oblong of yellow.

The meandering thoughts kept passing by my mind's eye, but very clearly there was also Pete's study. I was there, looking over the bookshelves, wishing I dared remove his books in order to put my own away neatly. Thinking of Laura and her nightmare. Wondering where Caesar was, had I left the basement light on, going to the door to whistle, imagining Janet asleep with her arm up over her head, if I slept like that my hands would go to sleep, whistling again for Caesar. Aware of the dog, although he was across the yard staring intently up a tree bole where a possum clung motionlessly. Everything a jumble, the bookshelves, the basement workshop, Janet, Caesar, driving down from Connecticut, pawing through drawers in the lab shop, looking for the sleeve controls, dots and dashes on slides . . .

I whistled once more and stepped down the first of the three steps to the yard, and fell. . . .

Falling forever, ice cold, tumbling over and over, with the knowledge that the fall would never end, would never change, stretching out for something, anything to grasp, to stop the tumbling. Nothing. Then a scream, and opening my eyes, or finding my eyes open. The light was no longer on.

Who screamed?

Everything was quiet, the gentle sound of the water on rocks, a rustling of a small creature in the grasses at the edge of the brook, an owl far back on the hill. There was a September chill in the air suddenly and I was shivering as I hurried back to my house.

I knew that I hadn't fallen asleep. Even if I had dozed

momentarily, I couldn't have been so deeply asleep that
I could have had a nightmare. Like Laura's, I thought,
and froze. Is that what she had dreamed? Falling forever? There had been no time. During the fall I knew that I
had been doing it for an eternity, that I would continue
to fall for all the time to come.

Janet's body was warm as she snuggled up to me, and
I clung to her almost like a child, grateful for this
long-limbed, practical woman.

We met our new neighbor on Saturday. Janet made a
point of going over to introduce herself and give her an
invitation for a drink, or coffee. "She's so small," Janet
said. "About thirty, or a little under. And handsome in a
strange way. In spite of herself almost. You can see that
she hasn't bothered to do anything much about her
appearance, I mean she has gorgeous hair, or could
have, but she keeps it cut about shoulder length and lets
it go at that. I bet she hasn't set it in years. Same for her
clothes. It's as if she never glanced in a mirror, or a
fashion magazine, or store window. Anyway, you'll see
for yourself. She'll be over at about four."

There was always work that needed doing immediately in the yard, and on the house or the car, and generally
I tried to keep Saturday open to get some of it done.
That day I had already torn up the television, looking for
the source of the fuzzy sound, and I had replaced a tube
and a speaker condenser, but it still wasn't the greatest.
Rusty wanted us to be hooked up to the cable, and I was
resisting. From stubbornness, I knew. I resented having
to pay seventy-five dollars in order to bring in a picture
that only three years ago had been clear and sharp. A
new runway at the airport had changed all that. Their
radar and the flight paths of rerouted planes distorted
our reception. But I kept trying to fix it myself.

Janet was painting window shades for Laura's room.
She had copied the design from some material that she
was using for a bedspread and drapes. She had baked

two pies, and a cake, and a loaf of whole-wheat bread.
The house was clean and smelled good and we were
busy. And happy. It always sounds hokey to say that
you're a happy man. Why aren't you tearing out your
hair over the foreign mess, or the tax problem, or some
damn thing? But I was a happy man. We had a good
thing, and knew it. Janet always baked on Saturday,
froze the stuff and got it out during the week, so the kids
hardly even knew that she was a working mother. They
were happy kids.

Then Christine came along. That's the only way to put
it. That afternoon she came up through the woods,
dressed in brown jeans, with a sloppy plaid shirt that
came down below her hips and was not terribly clean.
Laura ran down to meet her, and she was almost as big
as Christine.

"Hi," Janet said, coming out to the terrace. "Mrs.
Rudeman, this is Eddie. And Rusty."

"Please, call me Christine," she said, and held out her
hand.

But I knew her. It was like seeing your first lover again
after years, the same shock low in the belly, the same
tightening up of muscles, the fear that what's left of the
affair will show, and there is always something left over.
Hate, love, lust. Something. Virtually instantaneous
with the shock of recognition came the denial. I had
never seen her before in my life, except that one
morning on the way to work, and certainly I hadn't felt
any familiarity then. It would have been impossible to
have known her without remembering, if only because
of her size. You remember those who aren't in the range
of normality. She was possibly five feet tall, and couldn't
have weighed more than ninety pounds. It was impossible to tell what kind of a figure she had, but what was
visible seemed perfectly normal, just scaled down,
except her eyes, and they looked extraordinarily large in
so tiny a face. Her eyes were very dark, black or so close
to it as to make no difference, and her hair, as Janet had

said, was beautiful, or could have been with just a little attention. It was glossy, lustrous black, thick and to her shoulders. But she shouldn't have worn it tied back with a ribbon as she had it then. Her face was too round, her eyebrows too straight. It gave her a childlike appearance.

All of that and more passed through my mind as she crossed the terrace smiling, with her hand outstretched. And I didn't want to touch her hand. I knew that Janet was speaking, but I didn't hear what she said. In the same distant way I knew that Laura and Rusty were there, Laura waiting impatiently for the introductions to be over so she could say something or other. I braced myself for the touch, and when our fingers met, I knew there had been no way I could have prepared myself for the electricity of that quick bringing together of flesh to flesh. For God's sake, I wanted to say, turn around and say something to Rusty, don't just stand there staring at me. Act normal. You've never seen me before in your life and you know it.

She turned quickly, withdrawing her hand abruptly, but I couldn't tell if she had felt anything, or suspected my agitation. Janet was oblivious of any currents.

"But you and Rusty and Laura have all met," she said. "I keep forgetting how great kids are at insinuating themselves into any scene."

"Where's Caesar?" Laura finally got to ask.

I had another shock with the name. My nightmare, my waking nightmare. Or had I heard her calling to the dog?

"I never take him with me unless he's been invited," Christine said. "You never know where you'll run into a dog-hater, or a pet cat, or another dog that's a bit jealous."

They talked about the dog we had had until late in the spring, a red setter that had been born all heart and no brain. He had been killed out on the county road. Again I was distantly aware of what they were saying, almost as if I were half asleep in a different room, with voices

droning on and on beyond the walls. I was simply waiting for a chance to leave without being too rude.

The kids wandered away after a little while, and Janet and Christine talked easily. I began to listen when she mentioned Pete's name.

"Pete and Grace had been my husband's friends for a long time. Pete studied under him, and Grace and I were in classes together. So they invited me to stay in their house this year. Karl suggested Pete for the exchange program three years ago. He didn't believe there was a coherent American school of philosophy, and he thought that it would be good for Pete to study under the Cambridge system of Logical Positivism." She shrugged. "I take it that Pete didn't write to you and warn you that I'd be moving in. He said he would, but I guess I didn't really think he'd get around to it."

Karl Rudeman. Karl Rudeman. It was one of those vaguely familiar names that you feel you must know and can't associate with anything.

Janet had made a pitcher of gin and bitter lemon, and I refilled our glasses while I tried to find a tag to go with the name. Christine murmured thanks, then said, "It isn't fair that I should know so much about you both—from Pete—and that you know nothing about me. Karl was a psychologist at Harvard. He worked with Leary for several years, then they separated, violently, over the drugs. He died last May."

I felt like a fool then, and from the look on her face, I assumed that Janet did too. Karl Rudeman had won the Nobel for his work in physiological psychology, in the field of visual perception. There was something else nagging me about the name, some elusive memory that went with it, but it refused to come.

Christine stayed for another half hour, refused Janet's invitation to have dinner with us, and then went back home. Back through the woods, the way she had come.

"She's nice," Janet said. "I like her."

"You warn her about Glaser?"

"She's not interested. And it does take two. Anyway

she said that Pete gave her the rundown on everyone on the lane. You heard her."

"Yeah," I lied. I hadn't heard much of anything anyone had said. "He must have been thirty years older than she is."

"I suppose. I always wonder how it is with a couple like that. I mean, was he losing interest? Or just one time a month? Did it bother her?" Since Janet and I always wondered about everyone's sex life, that wasn't a strange line for our talk to have taken, but I felt uncomfortable about it, felt as if this time we were peeking in bedroom-door keyholes.

"Well, since you seem so sure she wouldn't be interested in Bill Glaser, maybe she's as sexual as she looked in that outfit."

"Hah!" That's all, just one Hah! And I agreed. We let it drop then.

We had planned a movie for that night. "Get some hamburgers out for the kids and I'll take you around to Cunningham's for dinner," I said to Janet as she started in with the tray. She looked pleased.

We always had stuffed crab at Cunningham's, and Asti Spumante. It's a way of life. Our first date cost me almost a week's pay, and that's what we did, so I don't suggest it too often, just a couple of times a year when things have suddenly clicked, or when we've had a fight and made up to find everything a little better than it used to be. I don't know why I suggested it that night, but she liked the idea, and she got dressed up in her new green dress that she had been saving for a party.

When I made love to her late that night, she burst into tears, and I stroked her hair until she fell asleep. I remembered the first time she had done that, how frightened I'd been, and her convulsive clutching when I had tried to get up to bring her a drink of water or something. She hadn't been able to talk, she just sobbed and held me, and slowly I had come to realize that I had a very sexy wife whose response was so total that it

overwhelmed her, and me. She sighed when I eased my
numb arm out from under her. Pins-and-needles circu-
lation began again and I rubbed my wrist trying to
hurry it along.

Christine Warnecke Rudeman, I thought suddenly.
Christine Warnecke. Of course. The photographer.
There had been a display of her pictures at the library a
year or two ago. She had an uncanny way of looking at
things, as if she were at some point that you couldn't
imagine, getting an angle that no one ever had seen
before. I couldn't remember the details of the show, or
any of the individual pieces, only the general impression
of great art, or even greater fakery. I could almost
visualize the item I had read about the death of her
husband, but it kept sliding out of focus. Something
about his death, though. Something never explained.

Tuesday I went home for lunch. I often did, the lab
was less than a mile from the house. Sometimes I took
Lenny with me, but that day he was too busy with a
printed circuit that he had to finish by six and he nodded
without speaking when I asked if he wanted a sandwich.
The air felt crisp and cool after the hot smell of solder as
I walked home.

I was thinking of the computer cutting tool that we
were finishing up, wondering if Mike had mastered the
Morse code yet, anticipating the look on his face when I
installed the ham set. I was not thinking of Christine,
had, in fact, forgotten about her, until I got even with
the house and suddenly there she was, carrying a tripod
out toward a small toolhouse at the rear of the lot.

I turned in the Donlevy drive. If it had been Ruth
Klinger, or Grace Donlevy, or any of the other women
who lived there, I would have offered a hand. But as
soon as I got near her, I knew I'd made a mistake. It hit
me again, not so violently, but still enough to shake me
up. I know this woman, came the thought.

"Hi, Eddie." She put the tripod down and looked hot

and slightly out of breath. "I always forget how heavy it can get. I had it made heavy purposely, so it could stay in place for months at a time, and then I forget."

I picked it up and it was heavy, but worse, awkward. The legs didn't lock closed, and no matter how I shifted it, one of them kept opening. "Where to?" I asked.

"Inside the toolshed. I left the door open. . . ."

I positioned it for her and she was as fussy as Lenny got over his circuits, or as I got over wiring one of the suits. It pleased me that she was that fussy about its position at an open window. I watched her mount a camera on the tripod and again she made adjustments that were too fine for me to see that anything was changed. Finally she was satisfied. All there was in front of the lens was a maple tree. "Want to take a look?" she asked.

The tree, framed by sky. I must have looked blank.

"I have a timer," she said. "A time-lapse study of the tree from now until spring, I hope. If nothing goes wrong."

"Oh." My disappointment must have shown.

"I won't show them side by side," she said, almost too quickly. "Sort of superimposed, so that you'll see the tree through time. . . ." She looked away suddenly and wiped her hands on her jeans. "Well, thanks again."

"What in hell do you mean, through time?"

"Oh . . . Sometime when you and Janet are free I'll show you some of the sort of thing I mean." She looked up, apologetically, and shrugged as she had that first time I met her. It was a strange gesture from one so small. It seemed that almost everything was too much for her, that when she felt cornered she might always simply shrug off everything with that abrupt movement.

"Well, I have to get," I said then, and turned toward the drive. "Do you have anything else to lug out here, before I leave?"

"No. The timer and film. But that's nothing. Thanks again." She took a step away, stopped and said, with that

same shy apologetic tone, "I wish I could explain what I want to do, in words. But I can't."

I hurried away from her, to my own house, but I didn't want anything to eat after all. I paced the living room, into the kitchen, where the coffee I had poured was now cold, back to the living room, out to the terrace. I told myself asinine things like: I love Janet. We have a good life, good sex, good kids. I have a good business that I am completely involved in. I'm too young for the male climacteric. She isn't even pretty.

And I kept pacing until I was an hour later than I'd planned on. I still hadn't eaten, and couldn't, and I forgot to make the sandwich for Lenny and take it back to him.

I avoided Christine. I put in long hours at the lab, and stayed in the basement workshop almost every evening, and turned down invitations to join the girls for coffee, or talk. They were together a lot. Janet was charmed by her, and a strong friendship grew between them rapidly. Janet commented on it thoughtfully one night. "I've never had many woman friends at all. I can't stand most women after a few minutes. Talking about kids sends me right up the wall, and you know how I am about PTA and clubs and that sort of thing. But she's different. She's a person first, then a woman, and as a person she's one of the most interesting I've ever run into. And she has so much empathy and understanding. She's very shy, too. You never have to worry about her camping on your doorstep or anything like that."

She'd been there almost two months when Pete's letter finally arrived telling us about her. Janet read it aloud to me while I shaved.

" 'She's a good kid and probably will need a friend or two by the time she gets out of that madhouse in Connecticut. Rudeman was a genius, but not quite human. Cold, calculating, never did a thing by accident in his life. He wound her up every morning and gave her instructions for the day. God knows why she married

him, why they stayed together, but they did. In his own way I think Rudeman was very much in love with her. He said once that if he could understand this one woman he'd understand the entire universe. May he rest in peace, he never made it. So be good to her.

"'Grace sends love. She's been redoing our apartment. . . .'"

I stopped listening. The letter went on for three pages of single-spaced typing. The letter had left as many questions as it had answered. More in fact, since we already had found out the basic information he had supplied. I decided to go to the library and look up Rudeman and his death and get rid of that nagging feeling that had never gone away.

"Eddie, for heaven's sake!" Janet was staring at me, flushed, and angry.

"What? Sorry, honey. My mind was wandering."

"I noticed. What in the world is bothering you? You hear me maybe half the time, though I doubt it."

"I said I'm sorry, Janet. God damn it!" I blotted a nick and turned to look at her, but she was gone.

She snapped at Rusty and Laura, and ignored me when I asked if there was any more mail. Rusty looked at me with a What's-eating-her? expression.

I tried to bring up the subject again that night, and got nowhere. "Nothing," she said. "Just forget it."

"Sure. That suits me fine." I didn't know what I was supposed to forget. I tried to remember if it was time for her period, but I never knew until it hit, so I just left her in the kitchen and went downstairs to the workroom and messed around for an hour. When I went back up, she was in bed, pretending to be asleep. Usually I'd keep at it until we had it out in the open, whatever it was, and we'd both explain our sides, maybe not convincing each other, but at least demonstrating that each thought he had a position to maintain. That time I simply left the bedroom and wandered about in the living room, picked up a book to read, put it down again. I found Pete's letter and saw that we'd been invited to visit them

over Christmas. I seemed to remember that Janet had gone on about that, but I couldn't recall her words. Finally I pulled on a jacket and walked out to the terrace. I looked toward the Donlevy house, Christine's house now. Enough leaves had fallen by then so I could see the lights.

It's your fault, I thought at her. Why don't you beat it? Go somewhere else. Go home. Anywhere else. Just get out.

I was falling. Suddenly there was nothing beneath my feet, nothing at all, and I was falling straight down in a featureless grey vacuum. I groped wildly for something to hold on to, and I remembered the last time it had happened, and that it had happened to Laura. Falling straight down, now starting to tumble, my stomach lurching, nausea welling up inside me. Everything was gone, the house, terrace, the lights. . . . I thought hard of the lights that had been the last thing I had seen. Eyes open or closed, the field of vision didn't change, nothing was there. "Janet!" I tried to call, and had no way of knowing if I had been able to make the sound or not. I couldn't hear myself. A second sweep of nausea rose in me, and this time I tasted the bitterness. I knew that I would start crying. I couldn't help it; nausea, fear, the uncontrollable tumbling, unable to call anyone. Fury then displaced the helplessness that had overcome me, and I yelled, again without being able to hear anything, "You did this, didn't you, you bitch!"

Donlevy's study was warm, the colors were dull gold, russet, deep, dark green. There was a fire in the fireplace. The room was out of focus somehow, not exactly as I remembered it, the furniture too large and awkward-looking, the shelves built to the ceiling were too high, the titles on the topmost shelf a blur because of the strange angle from which I saw them. Before me was Donlevy's desk, cleaner than I'd ever seen it, bare with gleaming wood, a stand with pens, and several sheets of paper. No stacks of reports, journals, overflowing ashtrays . . . I looked at the papers curiously, a

letter, in a neat legible handwriting. Two pages were turned face down, and the third was barely begun: ". . . nothing to do with you in any way. When I have finished going through the papers, then I'll box up those that you have a right to and mail them to you. It will take many weeks, however, so unti . . ." The last word ended with a streak of ink that slashed downward and across the page, and ran off onto the desktop.

Where was she, Christine? How had I got . . . I realized that I wasn't actually there. Even as the thought formed, I knew precisely where I was, on my own terrace, leaning against a post, staring at the lights through the bare trees.

I looked at the letter, and slowly raised my hand and stared at it, both on the terrace and in the study. And the one in the study was tiny, tanned, with oval nails, and a wide wedding band. . . .

"Eddie?"

Janet's voice jolted me, and for a moment the study dimmed, but I concentrated on it, and held it. "Yes."

"Are you all right?"

"Sure. I thought you were sleeping."

In the study . . . who the devil was in the study? Where was *she*? Then suddenly she screamed, and it was both inside my head and outside filling the night.

"My God!" Janet cried. "It's Christine! Someone must have . . ."

I started to run toward her house, the Donlevy house, and Janet was close behind me in her robe and slippers. In the split second before that scream had exploded into the night, I had been overcome by a wave of terror such as I had never known before. I fully expected to find Christine dead, with her throat cut, or a bullet in her brain, or something. Caesar met us and loped with us to the house, yelping excitedly. Why hadn't he barked at a stranger? I wanted to kick the beast. The back door was unlocked. We rushed in, and while Janet hesitated, I dashed toward the study.

Christine was on the floor near the desk, but she

wasn't dead, or even injured as far as I could tell from a hurried examination. Janet had dropped to her knees also, and was feeling the pulse in Christine's wrist, and I saw again the small tanned hand that I had seen only a few minutes ago, even the wedding band. The terror that had flooded through me minutes ago surged again. How could I have dreamed of seeing that hand move as if it were my own hand? I looked about the study frantically, but it was back to normal, nothing distorted now. I had been dreaming, I thought, dreaming. I had dreamed of being this woman, of seeing through her eyes, feeling through her. A dream, no more complicated than any other dream, just strange to me. Maybe people dreamed of being other people all the time, and simply never mentioned it. Maybe everyone walked around terrified most of the time because of inexplicable dreams. Christine's eyelids fluttered, and I knew that I couldn't look at her yet, couldn't let her look at me. Not yet. I stood up abruptly. "I'll have a look around. Something scared her."

I whistled for Caesar to come with me, and we made a tour of the house, all quiet, with no signs of an intruder. The dog sniffed doors, and the floor, but in a disinterested manner, as if going through the motions because that was expected of him. The same was true of the yard about the house; he just couldn't find anything to get excited about. I cursed him for being a stupid brute, and returned to the study. Christine was seated on one of the dark green chairs, and Janet on one facing her. I moved casually toward the desk, enough to see the letter, to see the top lines, the long streak where the pen had gone out of control.

Janet said, "Something must have happened, but she can't remember a thing."

"Fall asleep? A nightmare?" I suggested, trying not to look at her.

"No. I'm sure not. I was writing a letter, in fact. Then suddenly there was something else in the room with me. I know it. It's happened before, the same kind of feeling,

and I thought it was the farmhouse, the associations there. But maybe I am going crazy. Maybe Victor's right, I need care and treatment." She was very pale, her eyes so large that she looked almost doll-like, an idealized doll-like face.

"Who is Victor?" Janet asked.

"Eugenia's husband. She's . . . she was my husband's daughter." Christine sighed and stood up, a bit unsteadily. "If it starts again . . . I thought if I just got away from them all, and the house . . . But if it starts again here . . ."

"Eddie, we can't leave her like this," Janet said in a low voice. "And we can't leave the kids alone. Let's take her home for the night."

Christine objected, but in the end came along through the woods with Janet and me. At our house Janet went to get some clothes on. Her gown and robe had been soaked with dew. While Janet was dressing, I poked up a fire in the fireplace, and then made some hot toddies. Christine didn't speak until Janet came back.

"I'm sorry this happened," she said then. "I mean involving you two in something as . . . as messy as this is."

Janet looked at me, waiting, and I said, "Christine, we heard from Pete and he seemed to think you might need friends. He seemed to think we might do. Is any of this something that you could talk to Pete about?"

She nodded. "Yes. I could tell Pete."

"Okay, then let us be the friends that he would be if he was here."

Again she nodded. "Lord knows I have to talk to someone, or I'll go as batty as Victor wants to believe I am."

"Why do you keep referring to him?" Janet asked. Then she shook her head firmly. "No. No questions. You just tell us what you want to for now."

"I met Karl when I was a student at Northwestern. He had a class in physiological psychology and I was one of his students and experimental subjects. He was doing

his basic research then on perception. Three afternoons a week we would meet in his lab for tests that he had devised, visual-perception tests. He narrowed his subjects down to two others and me, and we are the ones he based much of his theory on. Anyway, as I got to know him and admire him more and more, he seemed to take a greater interest in me. He was a widower, with a child, Eugenia. She was twelve then." Her voice had grown fainter, and now stopped, and she looked at the drink in her hand that she had hardly touched. She took a sip, and another. We waited.

"The reason he was interested in me, particularly, at least in the beginning," she said haltingly, "was that I had been in and out of institutions for years." She didn't look up and her words were almost too low to catch. "He had developed the theory that the same mechanism that produces sight also produces images that are entirely mental constructs, and that the end results are the same. In fact, he believed and worked out the theory that all vision, whether or not there is an external object, is a construct. Vision doesn't copy anything in the real world, but instead involves the construction of a schematic, and so does visual imagination, or hallucination."

I refilled our glasses and added a log to the fire, and she talked on and on. Rudeman didn't believe in a psychological cause to explain schizophrenia, but believed it was a chemical imbalance with an organic cause that produced aberrated perception. This before the current wave of research that seemed to indicate that he had been right. His interest in Christine had started because she could furnish information on image projection, and because in some areas she had an eidetic memory, and this, too, was a theory that he was intensely interested in. *Eidetikers* had been discounted for almost a century in the serious literature, and he had reestablished the authenticity of the phenomena.

"During the year," she said, "he found out that there were certain anomalies in my vision that made my value

to him questionable. Gradually he had to phase me out, but he became so fascinated in those other areas that he couldn't stand not starting another line of research immediately, using me extensively. That was to be his last year at Northwestern. He had an offer from Harvard, and he was eager to go there. Anyway, late in April that year I . . . I guess I flipped out. And he picked up the pieces and wouldn't let me go to a psychiatrist, but insisted on caring for me himself. Three months later we were married."

Janet's hand found mine, and we listened to Christine like that, hand in hand.

"He was very kind to me," Christine said slowly sometime during that long night. "I don't know if he loved me, but I think I would have died without him. I think—or thought—that he cured me. I was well and happy, and busy. I wanted to take up photography and he encouraged it and made it possible. All those years he pursued a line of research that he never explained to me, that he hadn't published up to the time of his death. I'm going through his work now, trying to decode it, separating personal material from the professional data."

She was leaving out most of it, I believed. Everything interesting, or pertinent, or less than flattering to her she was skipping over. Janet's hand squeezed mine; take it easy, she seemed to be saying. Christine was obviously exhausted, her enormous eyes were shadowed, and she was very pale. But, damn it, I argued with myself, why had she screamed and fainted? How had her husband died?

"Okay," Janet said then, cheerfully, and too briskly. "Time's up for now. We'll talk again tomorrow, or the next day, or whenever you're ready to, Christine. Let me show you your room." She was right, of course. We were all dead tired, and it was nearly three, but I resented stopping it then. How had her husband died?

She and Janet left and I kicked at the feeble fire and finished my last drink, gathered up glasses and emptied

ashtrays. It was half an hour before Janet came back. She looked at the clock and groaned.

"Anything else?"

She went past me toward the bedroom, not speaking until we were behind the closed door. "It must have been gruesome," she said then, starting to undress. "Victor and Eugenia moved in with her. Karl's daughter and son-in-law. And Karl's parents live there, too. And right away Victor began to press for Karl's papers. They worked together at the university. Then he began to make passes, and that was too much. She packed up and left."

I had finished undressing first, and sat on the side of the bed watching her. The scattering of freckles across her shoulders was fading now, her deep red tan was turning softly golden. I especially loved the way her hip bones showed when she moved, and the taut skin over her ribs when she raised her arms to pull her jersey over her head. She caught my look and glanced at her watch pointedly. I sighed. "What happened to her tonight?"

"She said that before she finally had to leave the farm up in Connecticut, the last night there, Victor came into her third-floor room and began to make advances—her word, by the way. She backed away from him, across the room and out onto a balcony. She has acrophobia, and never usually goes out on that balcony. But she kept backing up, thinking of the scandal if she screamed. Her stepdaughter's husband, after all. In the house were Karl's mother and father, Eugenia. . . . Victor knew she would avoid a scene if possible. Then suddenly she was against the rail and he forced her backward, leaning out over it, and when she twisted away from him, she looked straight down, and then fainted. She said that tonight she somehow got that same feeling, she thinks that that memory flooded back in and that she lived that scene over again, although she can't remember anything except the feeling of looking down and falling. She screamed and fainted, just like that other night." Janet slipped into bed. "I think I reassured her a little bit

anyway. If that's what happened, it certainly doesn't mean she's heading for another break. That's the sort of thing that can happen to anyone at any time, especially where one of those very strong phobias is concerned."

I turned off the light, and we lay together, her cheek on my shoulder, her left arm across my chest, her left leg over my leg. And I thought of Christine in the other room under the same roof. And I knew that I was afraid of her.

The next morning was worse than usual. Thank God it's Friday, we both said a number of times. I had no desire to see Christine that morning, and was relieved that she seemed to be sleeping late. I told Janet I'd leave a note and ask her to go out by the side door, which would latch after her. But when the kids left to catch their bus, she came out.

"I wasn't sure if you'd told them that I was here. I thought it would complicate things to put in an appearance before they were gone," she said apologetically. "I'll go home now. Thanks for last night. More than I can say."

"Coffee?"

She shook her head, but I was pouring it already and she sat down at the kitchen table and waited. "I must look like hell," she said. She hadn't brought her purse with her, her long hair was tangled, she had no makeup on, and her eyes were deeply shadowed with violet. I realized that she was prettier than I had thought at first. It was the appeal of a little girl, however, not the attraction of a grown woman.

She sipped the coffee and then put the cup down and said again, "I'll go home now. Thanks again."

"Want a lift to your house? I have to leave too."

"Oh, no. That would be silly. I'll just go back through the woods."

I watched her as far as I could make out the small figure, and then I turned off lights and unplugged the coffee pot and left. But I kept seeing that slight unkempt

figure walking from me, toward the woods, tangled black hair, a knit shirt that was too big, jeans that clung to her buttocks like skin. Her buttocks were rounded, and moved ever so slightly when she walked, almost like a boy, but not quite; there was a telltale sway. And suddenly I wondered how she would be. Eager, actively seeking the contact, the thrust? Passive? I swerved the car, and tried to put the image out of mind, but by the time I had parked and greeted Lenny, I was in a foul mood.

Lenny always left the mail to me, including anything addressed to him that came in through the lab. In his name I had dictated three refusals of offers to join three separate very good firms. That morning there was the usual assortment of junk, several queries on prices and information, and an invitation to display our computer cutting tool and anything else of interest in the Chicago Exposition of Building Trades. Lenny smiled. We talked for an hour about what to show, how best to display it, and so on, and finally came down to the question we'd both been avoiding. Who would go? Neither of us wanted to. We finally flipped a coin and I lost.

I called Janet at the hospital and told her, and she suggested that we have some literature printed up, ready to hand out, or to leave stacked for prospective buyers to pick up.

"We should have literature," I called to Lenny, who nodded. "We can have a sketch of the machine, I guess," I said to Janet.

"Don't be silly. Let Christine take some pictures for you."

"Our neighbor, Christine Warnecke, would probably take pictures for us," I told Lenny. He nodded a bit more enthusiastically.

We scheduled the next two weeks as tightly as possible, planning for eighteen-hour days, trying to keep in mind the commitments we already had. We had to get a machine ready to take to Chicago, get it polished for photographs, get an assortment of programs for the

computer, keep the running check on the wired suits in the hospital cases, finish installing a closed-circuit TV in a private school, and so on.

I was late for dinner, and when I got there Janet simply smiled when I muttered, "Sorry."

"I know," she said, putting a platter of fried chicken down. "I know exactly what it will be like for the next few weeks. I'll see you again for Thanksgiving, or thereabouts."

I kissed her. While I was eating, the telephone rang. Christine, wondering if we'd like to see some of the work she'd done in the past few years. I remembered her offer to show us, but I shook my head at Janet. "Can't. I've got to write up the fact sheet tonight and be ready for the printers. They can take it Thursday. Did you mention the picture to her?" I motioned to the phone. Janet shook her head. "I will.

"Hi, Christine. Sorry, but I've got things that I have to do tonight. Maybe Janet can. Listen, would you be willing to take a picture of a machine for us, Lenny and me? He's my partner." She said of course, and I told her that Janet would fill in the details and hung up. I shooed Janet out, and went downstairs. Hours later I heard her come back, heard the basement door open slightly as she listened to see if I was still there. I clicked my pen on my beer glass, and the door closed. For a couple of seconds I considered my wife, decided she was a good sort, and then forgot her as I made another stab at the information sheet.

By twelve thirty I had a workable draft. It would need some polish, and possibly some further condensation, but it seemed to be adequate. I went upstairs for a drink before going to bed. I didn't turn on the living-room lights, but sat in the darkened room and went over and over the plans we had made. Tomorrow I'd get Christine over to take the pictures. . . .

I suddenly saw her buttocks as she moved away from me, and her enormous eyes as she sat at the table and sipped coffee, and the very small hand with its wide

band of gold. I closed my eyes. And saw the hand again, this time it opened and closed before my face, turning over and over as I examined it. I saw the other hand, and it was as if it were my own hand. I could raise and lower it. I could touch the right one to the left one, lift one to . . . my face. I stared at the room, the guest room in the Donlevy house. I had slept there before. Janet and I had stayed there years ago while paint dried in our house. I knew I was seated in the darkened living room, with a rum collins in my hand, knew Janet was sleeping just down the hall, but still I was also in that other room, seeing with eyes that weren't my eyes.

I started to feel dizzy, but this time I rejected the thought of falling. *No!* The feeling passed. I lifted the hands again, and got up. I had been in a deep chair, with a book on my lap. It slipped off to the floor. I tried to look down, but my eyes were riveted, fixed in a straight-ahead stare. I ordered the head to move, and with a combination of orders and just doing it, I forced movement. I forced her-me to make a complete turn, so that I could examine the whole room. Outside, I ordered, and walked down the hall to the living room, to the study. There were other thoughts, and fear. The fear was like a distant surf, rising and falling, but not close enough to feel, or to hear actually. It grew stronger as the walk continued. Dizziness returned, and nausea. I rejected it also.

The nausea had to do with the way my eyes were focusing. Nothing looked normal, or familiar, if my gaze lingered on it. And there was movement where I expected none. I made her stop and looked at the study from the doorway. The desk was not the straight lines and straight edges that I had come to know, but rather a blur that suggested desk, that I knew meant desk, and that did mean desk if I closed my eyes, or turned from it. But while I looked at it, it was strange. It was as if I could look through the desk to another image, the same piece of furniture, but without the polish, without casters, the same desk at an earlier stage. And beyond that, a rough

suggestion of the same desk. And further, wood not yet assembled. Logs. A tree on a forest floor. A tree in full leaf. As I looked at the tree, it dwindled and went through changes: leaves turned color and fell and grew again, but fewer; branches shortened and vanished and the tree shrank and vanished. . . .

I jerked away, and in the living room my heart was pounding and I couldn't catch my breath. I waited for the next few minutes, wondering if I were having a heart attack, if I had fallen asleep, wondering if I were going mad. When I could trust my hands to move without jerking, I lifted the drink and swallowed most of it before I put it down again. Then I paced the living room for several minutes. Nothing had happened, I knew. Overtired, imaginative, half asleep, with vivid near-dreams. I refused to believe it was anything more than that. And I was afraid to try it again to prove to myself that that was all there was to it. I finished the drink, brushed my teeth, and went to bed.

Christine turned up at the shop at four the next afternoon. She shook Lenny's hand, businesslike and brisk, and thoroughly professional. He could have eaten her for breakfast without making a bulge. Her greeting to me was friendly and open. She looked very tired, as if she wasn't sleeping well.

"If you don't mind, Eddie, maybe Mr. Leonard can help me with the machine. I find that I work better with strangers than with people I know."

That suited me fine and I left them alone in the far end of the lab. Now and again I could hear Lenny's rumbling voice protesting something or other, and her very quiet answers. I couldn't make out her words, but from his I knew that she insisted on positioning the machine on a black velvet hanging for a series of shots. I groaned. Glamour yet.

"It's the contrast that I was after," she said when she was through. "The cold and beautifully functional machine, all shiny metal and angles and copper and plastic, all so pragmatic and wholesome, and open. Contrasted

by the mystery of black velvet. Like a sky away from the city lights. Or the bowels of a cave with the lights turned off. Or the deepest reaches of the mind where the machine was really born."

Right until the last I was ready to veto the velvet for background without even seeing it, but she got to me. It had been born in such a black bottomless void, by God. "Let's wait for proofs and then decide," I said. I wondered, had she looked at the machine, through it to the components, through them back to the idea as it emerged from the black? I tightened my hand on my mug and took a deep drink of the hot murky coffee. We probably had the world's worst coffee in the lab because Lenny insisted on making it and he never measured anything, or washed the pot. On the other hand, he seemed to think the stuff he turned out was good.

"I'll develop them later today and have proofs ready to show you tonight, if you want," Christine said to us.

"You want to pick them up and bring them in with you in the morning?" Lenny asked. I said sure, and Christine left. I didn't watch her walk away this time.

After dinner Janet and I both went over to her house to see the proofs. While I studied the pictures, Christine and Janet went to the kitchen to talk and make coffee. I finished and leaned back in my chair waiting for their return. Without any perceptible difference in my thoughts, my position, anything, I was seeing Janet through Christine's eyes. Janet looked shocked and unbelieving.

I stared at her and began to see other faces there, too. Younger, clearer eyes, and smoother-skinned, emptier-looking. I turned my head abruptly as something else started to emerge. I knew that if I had tried, I would have seen all the personality traits, including the ugliness, the pettiness, everything there was that went into her.

"What is it?" Janet asked, alarm in her voice.

I shook my head, *her* head. She tried to speak and I wouldn't let her. Without any warning I had crossed the

threshold of belief. I knew I could enter her, could use her, could examine whatever was in her mind without her being able to do anything about it. I knew in that same flash that she didn't realize what was happening, that she felt haunted, or crazy, but that she had no idea that another personality was inside her. I pulled away so suddenly that I almost let her fall down.

From the other room I heard Janet's cry, followed by the sound of breaking glass. I hurried to the kitchen to find her standing over Christine, who was sitting on a stool looking dazed and bewildered and very frightened.

"What's wrong?" I asked.

Janet shook her head. "I dropped a glass," she said, daring me not to believe.

I wondered why she lied to me, but leaving them alone again, I knew why. I had always been the rationalist in the family. I refused to grant the existence of ghosts, souls, spirits, unseen influences, astrology, palmistry, ESP, anything that couldn't be controlled and explained. I marveled at my absolute acceptance of what had happened. It was like seeing a puzzle suddenly take form and have meaning, like a child's puzzle where animals are hidden in line drawings; once you locate them, you can't lose them again. You know. I knew now. It happens once, you don't believe it; twice, you still don't believe. Three times, it's something you've known all your life. I knew. My hands were shaking when I lighted a cigarette, but inwardly I felt calmer than I had felt before as I considered Christine. I wasn't afraid of her any longer, for one thing. It was something I was doing, not something being done to me. I could control it. And she didn't know.

I stubbed out the cigarette and sat down abruptly. Rudeman? Had he lived in her mind throughout their marriage? Is that what drew him to her, made him marry a girl twenty-five years younger than he'd been. Had he managed to keep her by this—control? I couldn't use the word possession then. I wasn't thinking

of it as possession. It was more like having someone else's mind open for inspection, a tour for the curious, nothing more.

If I talked to her now, made her see what had happened, quite inadvertently, she could probably get help, learn how to control it so that future intrusion would be impossible. If Rudeman had cared for her at all, hadn't wanted to use her, he would have cured her, or had it done somehow. Maybe he had known, maybe that's what those boxes of books were about, the years of experimentation. A little human guinea pig, I thought. Large-eyed, frightened, trusting. Completely ignorant of what was being done to it. And over the image of the frightened woman came the image of her slight figure as she walked away from me toward the woods, with her little fanny swinging gracefully, the rest of her body a mystery under concealing clothes.

The way she saw things, there wouldn't be any mystery about anything. Into and through and out the other side. No wonder Rudeman had been fascinated. How did she manage to live with so many conflicting images? Did that explain her schizophrenia? Just a name they applied to a condition that was abnormal, without knowing anything about what it was actually? The questions were coming faster and faster, and the thought of her, sitting out there in the kitchen, with answers locked up under that skull, was too much. I began to pace. Not again. Not now especially, with Janet there. *She'd* begin to suspect me of being responsible, just as I had suspected her of being responsible long before I had an inkling of what was happening. I thought of Christine as *her*, with special emphasis on it, separating *her* from all other hers in the world, but not able or willing to think of her by name.

I wondered what they were doing in the kitchen. What was she telling Janet? I started through the hall toward the kitchen, then stopped, and hurriedly returned to the living room. I couldn't look at her yet. I had to think, to try to understand. I needed time to

accept all the way through what had happened between us. And I suddenly wondered what she saw when she looked at me, through me to all the things that I had always believed were invisible.

I couldn't stand being in that house any longer. I grabbed the proofs and stuffed them back into the envelope. In the hallway I yelled out to Janet, "I'm going back through the woods. I'll leave the car for you. Take your time."

She stuck her head out from the kitchen. I thought she looked at me with suspicion and coldness, but her words were innocuous, and I decided that I had imagined the expression. "I won't be much longer, honey. Be careful."

It was dark under the oak trees, with the tenacious leaves still clinging to the twigs, rustling in the wind. The ground was spongy and water came through my shoes quickly, ice cold, squishing with each step. A fine film of ice covered the two logs. I cursed as I slipped and slid across, thinking of the black frigid water below. At our side of the brook I paused and looked back at the glowing windows, and for just an instant I entered her. No transition now, just the sudden awareness of what she was seeing, what she was hearing, feeling, thinking. She moaned and fear throbbed in her temples. She shut her eyes hard. I got out as fast as I had entered, as shaken as she had been. I hadn't meant to do it. The thought and the act, if it could be called that, had been simultaneous. I rushed home, stumbling through the familiar woods, bumping into obstacles that seemed ominous: a log where yesterday the path had been clear, a hole covered with leaves, a trap to break an ankle in, a low branch that was meant to blind me, but only cut my cheek, a root that snaked out to lasso my foot, throwing me down face first into the ice-glazed leaves and dirt. I lay quietly for a minute. Finally I stood up and went on, making no attempt to brush off the muck. Muck and filth. It seemed fitting.

*   *   *

I still had a couple of hours of work to do that night. The following day Mike's body cast was being changed, and I had to be on hand. He had his ham operator's license, and Janet had said that the only problem now was that he didn't want to stop to sleep or eat or anything else. He was doing remarkably well in every way. She had kissed me with tears in her eyes when she reported. In the morning I had to drop the pictures off for Lenny, scoot over to the hospital, return for the pictures, take them back to her . . . I changed my mind. I'd let Lenny deliver the proofs. In fact, I wouldn't see *her* at all again. Ever.

I got in the tub and soaked for fifteen minutes, then put on pajamas and robe and went down to the basement to check out the program for Mike's computer. I didn't hear Janet come in, but when I went up at twelve thirty, she was in the living room waiting for me.

"I'm really concerned for her," she said. "I don't think she ought to be alone. And I don't think she's crazy, either."

"Okay. Tell." I headed for the kitchen and she followed. Janet had made coffee and it smelled good. I poured a cup and sat down.

"I don't know if I can or not," she said. "Christine has a gift of vision that I'm sure no one ever had before. She can see, or sense, the process of growth and change in things." I knew that I was supposed to register skepticism at that point, and I looked up at her with what I hoped was a prove-it expression. She became defensive. "Well, she can. She's trying to duplicate it with the camera, but she's very frustrated and disappointed in the results she's been able to get so far. She's got a new technique for developing time-lapse photographs. Whether or not it's what she is after, it's really remarkable. She prints a picture on a transparency, and shoots her next one through it, I think. When she prints that on another transparency, it gives the effect of being in layers, with each layer discernible, if you look hard enough. But she claims that for it to be successful, you

should be able to see each stage, with all the others a blur, each one coming into focus with the change in attention you give to it. And that's how she sees."

I finished the coffee and got up to pour a second cup, without commenting. Standing at the stove, with my back to her, I said, "I'm willing to believe that she's some kind of a genius. But, this other thing, the fainting, screams, whatever happened tonight. She needs a doctor."

"Yes. I know. I talked her into seeing Dr. Lessing. Lessing will be good to her." She made a short laughing sound, a snort of quickly killed mirth. "And he'll tell her to pick up a man somewhere and take him to bed. He thinks that widows and widowers shouldn't try to break the sex habit cold turkey." Again the tone of her voice suggested amusement when she added, "Knowing that she's coming to him through us, he'll probably recommend that she cultivate Lenny's company, two birds with one stone."

My hand was painfully tight on the cup handle. I remembered one night with Janet, saying, "Jesus, I wish I could be you just for once, just to see what happens to you when you cry like that, when you pass out, why that little smile finally comes through. . . ."

I knew my voice was too harsh then. I couldn't help it. I said, "I think she's a spook. I don't like being around her. I get the same feeling that I got when I was a kid around a great-uncle who had gone off the deep end. I was scared shitless of him, and I get the same feeling in the pit of my stomach when I'm near her."

"Eddie!" Janet moved toward me, but didn't make it all the way. She returned to her chair instead and sat down, and when she spoke again, her voice was resigned. Way back in Year One, we'd had an understanding that if ever either of us disliked someone, his feelings were to be respected without argument. It needed no rationalization: people liked or disliked other people without reason sometimes. And by throwing in a non-

existent uncle I had made double sure that she wouldn't argue with me. Finis. "Well," Janet said, "she certainly isn't pushy. If you don't want to be around her, you won't find her in your path."

"Yeah. And maybe later, after I get out from under all this other stuff, maybe I'll feel different. Maybe I'm just afraid right now of entanglement, because I'm too pressed for time as it is."

"Sure," Janet said. I liked her a lot right then, for the way she was willing to let me drop Christine, whom she had grown very fond of, and was intrigued by. She was disappointed that she had been cut off at the water, that she wouldn't be able now to talk about Christine, speculate about her. God knows, I didn't want to think about her any more than I had to from then on.

The next few days blurred together. I knew that things got done, simply because they didn't need doing later, but the memory of seeing to them, of getting them done, was gone. The geriatric patient came out of his cast on Saturday practically as good as new. He was walking again the same day they removed it, with crutches, but for balance, and to give him reassurance. His leg and hip muscles were fine. Lenny and I laughed and pounded each other over the back, and hugged each other, and split a bottle of Scotch, starting at one in the morning and staying with it until it was gone. He had to walk me home because neither of us could find a car key. Lenny spent the night, what was left of it. On Sunday I slept off a hangover and Lenny, Janet, the kids, and Christine all went for a long ride in the country and came back with baskets of apples, cider, black walnuts, and butternuts. And Janet said that Christine had invited all of us over for a celebration supper later on.

"I didn't say we'd come," Janet said. "I can call and say you still are hungover. I sort of hinted that you might be."

"Honey, forget it. How's Lenny? You should have seen him last night. He laughed!"

"And today he smiled a couple of times," she said, grinning. "He's over at Christine's house now, helping with firewood, or something."

"Tell her that we'll be over," I said.

The kids grumbled a little, but we got Mrs. Durrell in to sit and we went over to Christine's. Lenny was in the living room mixing something red and steaming in a large bowl. "Oh, God," I prayed aloud, "please, not one of his concoctions." But it was, and it was very good. Hot cider, applejack, brandy, and a dry red wine. With cinnamon sticks in individual cups.

Steaks, salad, baked potatoes, spicy hot apple pie. "If I knew you was coming," Christine had murmured, serving us, but she hadn't belabored the point, and it was a happy party. She proposed a toast after pouring brandy for us. "To the good men of the earth. Eddie and Lenny, and others like them wherever they are."

I knew that I flushed, and Lenny looked embarrassed and frowned, but Janet said, "Hear, hear," and the girls touched the glasses to their lips. In a few moments we were back to the gaiety that was interrupted by the toast that lingered in my head for the rest of the evening.

Lenny was more talkative than I'd seen him in years. He even mentioned that he had been a physicist, something that not more than a dozen people knew. The girls were both looking pretty after a day in the cold air; their cheeks were flushed, and they looked happy. Janet's bright blue-green eyes sparkled and she laughed easily and often. Christine laughed too, more quietly, and never at anything she said herself. She still was shy, but at ease with us. And it seemed that her shyness and Lenny's introspective quiet were well matched, as if there had been a meeting of the selves there that few others ever got to know. I caught Lenny's contemplative gaze on her once, and when she noticed also, she seemed to consider his question gravely, then she turned away, and the flush on her cheeks was a bit deeper. The air had changed somehow, had become more charged, and Janet's touch on my hand to ask for a

cigarette was a caress. I looked at her, acknowledging the invitation. Our hands lingered over the cigarette in the non-verbal communication that made living with her so nice.

I was very glad we had that evening together. Janet and I left at about twelve. Lenny was sitting in a deep chair before the fire when we said goodnight, and he made no motion to get up and leave then too. In our car Janet sighed and put her head on my shoulder.

Images flashed before my eyes: Christine's buttocks as she moved away from me; the tight skin across Janet's ribs when she raised her arms over her head; Christine's tiny, tiny waist, dressed as she had been that night, in a tailored shirt and black skirt, tightly belted with a wide leather belt; the pink nipples that puckered and stiffened at a touch; and darker nipples that I had never seen, but knew had to be like that, dark and large. And how black would her pubic hair be, and how hungry would she be after so long a time? Her head back, listening to a record, her eyes narrowed in concentration, her mouth open slightly. And the thought kept coming back: What would it be like to be her? What did Janet feel? What would *she* feel when Lenny entered her body? How different was it for a woman who was sexually responsive? She wouldn't even know, if I waited until she was thoroughly aroused. Sex had been in the air in the living room, we'd all felt it. After such a long period of deprivation, she'd crumble at Lenny's first touch. She'd never know, I repeated to myself.

When we got out of the car I said to Janet, "Get rid of Mrs. Durrell as fast as you can. Okay?" She pressed her body against mine and laughed a low, throaty laugh.

I was in a fever of anxiety then, trying to keep from going out into *her* too soon. Not yet. Not yet. Not until I had Janet in bed, not until I thought that *she* and Lenny had had time to be at ease with each other again after being left alone. Maybe even in bed. My excitement was contagious. Janet was in bed as soon as she could decently get rid of the sitter, and when my hand roamed

down her body, she shivered. Very deliberately I played
with her and when I was certain that she wouldn't
notice a shift in my attention, I went out to the other
one, and found her alone. My disappointment was so
great that momentarily I forgot about Janet, until her
sudden scream made me realize that I had hurt her. She
muffled her face against my chest and gasped, and
whether from pleasure or pain I couldn't tell, she didn't
pull away.

She was fighting eroticism as hard as she could.
Drawing up thoughts of plans, of work not yet finished,
of the notebooks that were so much harder to decipher
than she had suspected they would be, the time-lapse
photos that were coming along. Trying to push out of
her mind the ache that kept coming back deep in her
belly, the awful awareness of her stimulation from too
much wine, the nearness of Lenny and his maleness.
She was hardly aware of the intrusion this time, and
when I directed her thoughts toward the sensual and
sexual, there was no way she could resist. I cursed her
for allowing Lenny to leave, I threatened her, I forced
her to unfold when she doubled up like a foetus,
hugging herself into a tight ball. For an hour, more than
an hour, I made love to Janet and tormented that other
girl, and forced her to do those things that I had to
experience for myself. And when Janet moaned and
cried out, I knew the cause, and knew when to stop and
when to continue, and when she finally went limp, I
knew the total, final surrender that she knew. And I
stared at the mirror image of the girl: large dark nipples,
beautifully formed breasts, erect and rounded, deep
navel, black shiny hair. And mad eyes, haunted, panic-
stricken eyes in a face as white as milk, with two red
spots on her cheeks. Her breath was coming in quick
gasps. My control was too tight. Nothing that she
thought was coming through to me, only what she felt
with her body that had become so sensitive that when
she lay back on the bed, she shuddered at the touch of
the sheet on her back. I relaxed control without leaving

and there was a chaotic blur of memories, of nights in Karl's arms, of giving up totally to him, being the complete houri that he demanded of her.

"Bitch!" I thought at her. "Slut." I went on and on, calling her names, despising her for letting me do it to her, for being so manipulable, for letting me do this to myself. And I brought her to orgasm again, this time not letting her stop, or ease up, but on and on, until suddenly she arched her back and screamed, and I knew. I don't know if she screamed alone, or if I screamed with her. She blacked out, and I was falling, spinning around and around, plummeting downward. I yanked away from her. Janet stirred lazily against me, not awake, hardly even aware of me. I didn't move, but stared at the ceiling and waited for the blood to stop pounding in my head, and for my heart to stop the wild fibrillation that her final convulsion had started.

Janet was bright-eyed and pink the next morning, but when she saw the full ashtrays in the living room and kitchen, she looked at me closely. "You couldn't sleep?"

"Too much to think of," I said, cursing the coffee pot for its slowness. "And just four days to do it."

"Oh, honey." She was always regretful when I was awake while she slept. She felt it was selfish of her.

I could hardly bring myself to look at Lenny, but he took my moods in stride, and he made himself inconspicuous. The machine was gleaming and beautiful, ready to crate up and put in the station wagon. We wouldn't trust it to anyone but one of us, and I would drive to Chicago on Friday, install it myself Saturday morning, hours before the doors of the exposition opened at four in the afternoon. Lenny, like Janet, took my jittery state to be nerves from the coming show. It was like having a show at the Metropolitan, or a recital at Carnegie Hall, or a Broadway opening. And I wasn't even able to concentrate on it for a period of two consecutive minutes. I went round and round with the problem I had forced on myself by not leaving Christine Warnecke Rudeman strictly alone, and I couldn't find a

solution. I couldn't speak out now, not after last night. I couldn't advise her to seek help, or in any way suggest that I knew anything about her that she hadn't told us. And although the thoughts of the night before were a torture, I couldn't stop going over it all again and again, and feeling again the echo of the unbearable excitement and pleasures I had known. When Lenny left for lunch, I didn't even look up. And when he returned, I was still at the bench, pretending to be going over the installation plan we had agreed on for our space at the exposition. Lenny didn't go back to his own desk, or his work in progress on the bench. He dragged a stool across from me and sat down.

"Why don't you like Chris?" he asked bluntly.

"I like her fine," I said.

He shook his head. "No. You won't look at her, and you don't want her to look directly at you. I noticed last night. You find a place to sit where you're not in her line of sight. When she turns to speak to you, or in your direction, you get busy lighting a cigarette, or shift your position. Not consciously, Eddie. I'm not saying you do anything like that on purpose, but I was noticing." He leaned forward with both great hands flat on the bench. "Why, Eddie?"

I shrugged and caught myself reaching for my pack of cigarettes. "I don't know. I didn't realize I was doing any of those things. I haven't tried to put anything into words. I'm just not comfortable with her. Why? Are you interested?"

"Yes," he said. "She thinks she's going crazy. She is certain that you sense it and that's why you're uncomfortable around her. Your actions reinforce her feelings, giving you cause to be even more uncomfortable, and it goes on from there."

"I can keep the hell away from her. Is that what you're driving at?"

"I think so."

"Lenny," I said when he remained quiet, and seemed

lost in his speculations, "is she? Going crazy again? You know she was once?"

"No. I doubt it. She is different, and difference is treated like mental illness. That's what I know. No more. From demonic possession to witchcraft to mental illness. We do make progress." His hands, that had been flat and unmoving on the benchtop, bunched up into fists.

"Okay, Lenny," I said. "I believe you. And I won't see her any more for the next couple of weeks, whatever happens. And, Lenny, if I'd known—I mean, I didn't realize that anything of my attitude was coming through. I didn't really think about it one way or the other. I wouldn't do anything to hurt her . . . or you."

He looked at me gravely and nodded. "I know that," he said. He stood up and his face softened a bit. "It's always people like you, the rationalists, that are most afraid of any kind of mental disorders, even benign ones. It shows."

I shook my head. "A contradiction in terms, isn't that? Mental disorders and benign?"

"Not necessarily." Then he moved his stool back down the bench and went back to work. And I started at the sketches before me for a long time before they came back into focus. The rest of the afternoon I fought against going back to her and punishing her for complaining about me. I thought of the ways I could inflict punishment on her, and knew that the real ace that I would keep for an emergency was her fear of heights. I visualized strolling along the lip of the Grand Canyon with her, or taking her up the Empire State Building, the Eiffel Tower, or forcing her up the face of a cliff. And I kept a rigid control of my own thoughts so that I didn't go out to her at all. I didn't give in all week, but I had her nightmares.

On Wednesday Janet suggested that I should let Lenny go to Chicago and I snapped at her and called her a fool. On Thursday Lenny made the same suggestion, and I

stalked from the lab and drove off in a white fury. When Janet came home I accused them of getting together and talking about me.

"Eddie, you know better than that. But look at you. You aren't sleeping well, and you've been as nervous as a cat. What's the matter with you?"

"Just leave me alone, okay? Tired, that's all. Just plain tired. And tired of cross-examinations and dark hints and suspicions."

They were getting together, the three of them, all the time. I knew that Lenny was spending his evenings with Christine, and that Janet was with them much of the time when I was busy down in the basement workshop or out at the hospital. They said, Janet and Lenny, that they were trying to decipher the code that Karl Rudeman had used in making his notes. I didn't believe them.

They were talking about me, speculating on whether or not I was the one driving *her* crazy. I imagined the same conversation over and over, with Lenny insisting that I could have done *that* to her, and Janet, white-faced and frantic with indecision, denying it. Not while I had been with her, she would think. Not at a time like that.

Then I would snap awake, and either curse myself for being a fool, or become frightened by the paranoid drift of my thoughts. And I would know that none of it was true. Of course Janet wouldn't discuss what went on over there; I had practically forbidden her to do so. And Lenny wouldn't talk about it under the happiest circumstances, much less now.

Friday, driving to Chicago I began to relax, and after three hours on the road I was whistling and could almost forget the mess, could almost convince myself that I'd been having delusions, which was easier to take than the truth.

I slept deeply Friday night, and Saturday I was busy, getting our exhibit set up and getting acquainted with others who were also showing tools and machinery.

From four until the doors closed at eleven, the hall got fuller and fuller, the noise level became excruciating, the smoke-laden air unbreathable. Our cutting tool drew a good, interested response, and I was busy. And too tired for the late dinner I had agreed to with two other exhibitors. We settled for hamburgers and beer in the hotel dining room, and soon afterward I tumbled into bed and again slept like a child. The crowds were just as thick on Sunday, but by Monday the idle curiosity-seekers were back at their jobs, and the ones who came through were businesslike and fewer in number. I had hired a business student to spell me, and I left him in charge from four until seven, the slack hours, so I could have an early dinner and get some rest. But I found myself wandering the streets instead, and finally I stopped in front of a library.

Karl Rudeman, I thought. How did he die? And I went in and looked up the clippings about him, and read the last three with absorption. When I went to dinner afterward, I was still trying to puzzle it out. He had had dinner with his family: his wife, parents, daughter, and son-in-law. After dinner they had played bridge for an hour or two. Sometime after that, after everyone else had gone to bed, he had left the house to roam through the fields that stretched out for a quarter of a mile, down to the river. He had collapsed and died of a heart attack at the edge of a field. Christine, awakening later and finding him gone, had first searched the house, then, when she realized that Karl was in his pajamas and barefooted, she had awakened her stepson-in-law and started a search of the grounds. Karl wasn't found until daylight, and then the tenant farmer had been the one to spot the figure in orange-and-black striped pajamas. There was no sign of violence, and it was assumed that he had been walking in his sleep when the fatal attack occurred.

Back to the exhibit, and the flow of evening viewers. Invitations, given and accepted, for drinks later, and a beaver flick. Lunch with a couple of other men the

following day. A long talk with a manufacturer who was interested in procuring the order for the cutting tool, should there be enough interest to warrant it.

The obscene movie had been a mistake, I knew as soon as the girl jerked off her slip and opened her legs. Suddenly I was seeing *her*, open-legged on the edge of the bed before a mirror.

I pushed my way through a cluster of men at the back of the theater to get out into the cold November air again. I walked back to the hotel. A freezing mist was hanging head high, not falling, but just hanging there, and I gulped it in, thankful for the pain of the cold air in my throat. A prowl car slowed down as it passed me, it picked up speed again and moved on down the street. I had bought a stack of magazines and some paperbacks to read, but nothing in the room looked interesting when I took off my damp clothes and tried to persuade myself that I could fall asleep now.

I had room service send up a bottle of bourbon and ice, and tried to read a Nero Wolfe mystery. My attention kept wandering, and finally I lay back on the bed, balancing my drink on my stomach, and thought about *her*.

It was so easy, and gentle even. She didn't suspect this time, not at all. She was saying, ". . . because they're abstractions, you see. Emotions like fear, love, anger. First the physiological change in the brain, the electro-chemical changes that take place stimulating those abstractions, and then the experience of the emotion."

"You mean to say he really believed that the feeling of anger comes after the chemical changes that take place?"

"Of course. That's how it is with a physiological psychologist. And you can see it operate; tranquilizers permit you to know intellectually but they don't let you react, so you don't experience the anger or fear, or whatever."

Lenny was sitting back in the green chair in the study,

and she was behind the desk that was spread with snapshots and proofs.

"Okay. What triggers those changes in the first place?"

"Well, his specialty was sight, or vision, as he preferred to call it. Light entering the eye brings about a change in the chromophore in the first thousandth of a second, and after that the rest of the changes are automatic, a causal chain that results in the experiencing of a vision of some sort."

"I know," Lenny said gently. "But what about the vision that doesn't have an object in real space? The imaginary image? No light there to start the chain of events."

"A change brought about by electrochemical energy? The leakage of energy from cellular functioning? The first step is on a molecular level, not much energy is involved, after all. Lenny, it's happening . . ."

I got a jolt of fear then, along with the words spoken softly. Her hands clenched and a proof under her right hand buckled up and cracked. Before Lenny could respond, I pulled out and away.

I didn't know how she had found out, what I had done to give my presence away. But her knowledge had been as certain as mine, and the fear was named now, not the fear of insanity. It was a directed fear and hatred that I had felt, directed at me, not the aimless, directionless, more-powerful fear that my presence had stimulated before. She knew that something from outside had entered her. I sat up and finished my drink, then turned off the light. And I wondered what they had been finding in those notes. . . . Half a bottle and hours later I fell asleep.

I dreamed that I was being chased, that I kept calling back over my shoulder, "Stop, it's me! Look at me! It's me!" But it didn't stop, and steadily it gained ground, until I knew that I was going to be caught, and the thought paralyzed me. All I could do then was wait in

rigid, motionless, soundless terror for it to reach out and get me.

The nightmare woke me up, and it was minutes before I could move. It was nearly daylight; I didn't try to sleep any more. I was too afraid of having *her* dreams again. At seven thirty I called Janet.

"Hey," she said happily. "I thought we'd never hear from you."

"I sent some cards."

"But you'll be here before they will. How's it going?"

"Fine. Boring after the first day. I went to a dirty movie last night."

"I hope you had bad dreams. Serve you right." Her voice was teasing and cheerful and happy, and I could see her smile and the light in her eyes.

"How's everything there?" I couldn't ask about Lenny and Christine. If they had found out anything, they hadn't told her. I'd know, if they had. We chatted for several minutes, then she had to run, and I kissed her over the wire and we both hung up at the same time, the way we always did. I was being stupid. Naturally they wouldn't tell her. Hey, did you know that your husband's been torturing this woman psychologically, that he raped her repeatedly, that he's contemplating killing her? I jerked from the bed, shaking.

I had a dull pain behind my right eye when I went down to breakfast. A wind was driving sleet through the streets like sheer white curtains, and I stopped at the doorway, shivering, and went back inside to the hotel dining room. I couldn't think, and I knew that I had to think now.

If Lenny deciphered the notebooks, and if Karl had known that she could be possessed—there, I thought with some satisfaction, I used the word. If he had known and put that in his notebooks, then Lenny was bright enough to know that the recurrence of her schizophrenia was more than likely due to a new invasion. I groaned. He wouldn't believe that. *I* couldn't even believe it. No one in his right mind would, unless he had

done it and could prove it to himself. . . . I gripped my cup so hard that coffee splashed out and I had to use both hands to return the cup to the saucer. Had Lenny gone into her too?

The pain behind my eye was a knife blade now. Lenny! Of course. I tried to lift the coffee and couldn't. I flung down my napkin and got up and hurried back to my room, as fast as I could get out of there. I paced, but no matter how I came to it, I ended up thinking that the only way Lenny could have accepted the thing was through experience. First Rudeman, then me, and now Lenny.

He couldn't have her. She was mine now. And I would never give her up.

The pain was unbearable and I collapsed, sprawled across the bed, clutching my head. I hadn't had a migraine in years. It was not knowing. Not knowing how much they had found out, not knowing what they were doing, what they were planning, not knowing if there was a way they could learn about me.

I went to her abruptly, roughly. She dropped a pan of developer and moaned, and caught the sink in a dark room. "No!" she cried. "Please. No!"

I tried to make her remember everything Lenny had said to her, tried to bring back his voice, but there was too much, it came too fast. She was too frightened, and intermixed were the revived thoughts of insanity, of Karl's voice, Lenny's words. Too much. She had to relax. I took her to the couch and made her lie down and stop thinking. I felt her fear, and hatred, and abhorrence, like a pulse beating erratically, with each beat the pressure increased, and then ebbed. She tried to break away, and we struggled, and I hurt her. I didn't know what I had done, how I had managed it, but she groaned and wept and fell down again, and now my pain was also her pain. "Karl," she whispered soundlessly, "please go. Please leave me alone. I'm sorry. I didn't know. Please."

I stayed with her for more than an hour, and then I tried to force her to forget. To know nothing about my

presence. She struggled again, and this time she screamed piercingly, and for a moment the feeling of a plunge straight down was almost overwhelming, but everything stopped, and I could find nothing there to communicate with, nothing to probe. It was like being swallowed by a sea of feathers that stretched out in all directions, shifting when I touched them, but settling again immediately. She had fainted.

I fell asleep almost immediately and when I awakened it was nearly two, and my headache was gone. I went to the exposition.

That afternoon a man returned who had been at the stall for almost an hour on Saturday. He had a companion this time. "Hi, Mr. Laslow. Hendrickson, remember? Like you to meet Norbert Weill."

Of course, I knew who Norbert Weill was. If you had a home workshop, you had something of his in it. If you had a small commercial shop, you probably had something of his. If you had a hundred-man operation, you'd have something of his. He was about sixty, small and square, with muscles like a boxer's. He grunted at the introduction, his handshake was a no-nonsense test of strength. "Hendrickson says it'll cut through plastic, glass, aluminum, steel. Without changing nothing but the program. That right?"

"Yes. Would you like a demonstration?"

"Not here. In my shop. How much?"

"I can't discuss that without my partner, Mr. Weill."

"Get him, then. When can he make it?"

So it went. In the end I agreed to call Lenny, then get in touch with Weill again at his Chicago office. Lenny didn't sound very enthusiastic. "Let him have the machine in his own shop for a couple of weeks after you close down there. Then let him make an offer."

"I think he'll make the offer without all that, if we're both on hand to discuss it. Outright sale of this machine, an advance against royalties. Could come to quite a bundle."

"Christ! I just don't . . . Eddie, can you get away from that place for a couple of hours? I've got to have a talk with you. Not about this goddam machine, something else."

"Sure. Look, plan to fly up on Friday. It'll take an hour, no more. A couple of hours for the talk with Weill. A couple more with me, then fly back. Six hours is all. Or less maybe. You can afford to take one lousy day off."

"Okay. I'll call your hotel and let you know what time I'll get in." He sounded relieved.

"Hey, wait a minute. What the hell is going on? Is it one of the suits? The closed-circuit TV giving trouble? What?"

"Oh. Sorry, Eddie. I thought I said personal. Nothing at the shop. Everything's fine. It's . . . it's something with Chris. Anyway, see you Friday."

I didn't go back to the booth, but instead found a small coffee shop in the exposition building and sat there smoking and thinking about Lenny and Christine, and Janet and me, and Mr. Weill, and God knows what else. This was it, I thought, the break we'd been waiting for. I didn't doubt that. Money, enough for once to do the things we'd been wanting to do. A bigger shop, more equipment, maybe some help, even a secretary to run herd on books. And neither Lenny nor I cared. Neither of us gave a damn.

Sitting there, with coffee in front of me, a cigarette in my fingers, I probed Christine to see what was happening. She was talking in a low voice. Her eyes were closed. Going into her was like putting on distortion lenses, putting scrambling devices in my ears. Nothing was in clear focus, no thoughts were coherent all the way through. She was on something, I realized. Something that had toned down everything, taken off all the edges, all the sharpness.

"I used to walk on that same path, after . . . I saw the fields sown, the tractors like spiders, back and forth, back and forth, stringing a web of seeds. And the green shoots—they really do shoot out, like being released, a

rubber band that is suddenly let go, but they do it in slow motion. It was a wheat field. Pale green, then as high as my shoulders so that I was a head floating over the field, only a head. Magician's best trick. Float a head. Then the harvesters came and the snow fell. And it was the same walk. You see? And I couldn't tell which was the real one. They were all real. Are real. All of them are. The tranquilizers. He said I shouldn't take them. Have to learn how to find which one is now and concentrate on it. No tranquilizers."

She sighed, and the images blurred, fused, separated again. She turned off a tape recorder, but continued to lie still, with her eyes closed. Her thoughts were a chaotic jumble. If she suspected that I was there, she gave no indication. She was afraid to open her eyes. Trying to remember why she had walked along that path so many times after Karl died out there. In the beginning, the hours of training, hours and hours of testing. Then the experiments. Afraid of him. Terribly afraid. He had cleared the world for her, but he might scramble it again. So afraid of him. If she took the capsules and went to bed, it didn't matter, but now. Afraid to open her eyes. Lenny? Isn't it time yet? It's been so long—days, weeks. Snow has fallen, and the summer heat has come and gone. I know the couch is under me, and the room around me, and my finger on the switch to the recorder. I know that. I have to repeat it sometimes, but then I know it. Mustn't open my eyes now. Not yet. Not until Lenny comes back.

I smelled burning filter and put out the cigarette and drank coffee. What would she see if she opened her eyes now? Was that her madness? A visual distortion, a constant hallucination, a mixture of reality and fantasy that she couldn't tell apart? She turned her head, faced the back of the couch.

Very slowly I forced her to sit up, and then to open her eyes. It was much harder than making her respond had been before. She kept slipping away from me. It was as if there were so many other impulses that mine was

just one of a number, no more powerful than any of the illusory ones that kept holding up images for her to scan and accept, or reject. Finally she opened her eyes, and the room began to move. There was no sequence, no before and after, or cause and effect. Everything was. Winter, with a fire in the fireplace, summer with fans in the windows, company talking gaily, the room empty, children playing with puzzles, a couple copulating on the couch, a man pacing talking angrily . . . They were all real. I knew we—I had to get out of there, and there was no place to go. I was afraid of the outside world even more than the inside one. I was afraid to move. The couch vanished from behind me. The room was moving again. And I knew it would vanish, and that I would fall, like I had fallen a thousand times, a million times.

"Help me!" I cried to the pacing man, and he continued to pace although the room was certainly fading. And the children played. And the couple made love. And the fans whirred. And the fire burned. And I fell and fell and fell and fell. . . .

I sat in the coffee shop and shook. I was in a sweat, and I couldn't stop the shaking in my hands. I didn't dare try to walk out yet. No more! No more. I shook my head and swore, no more. I'd kill her. She had learned what to do, what not to do, and through my stupidity and blundering, I'd kill her.

"Sir? Is anything wrong? Are you all right?"

The waitress. She touched my arm warily, ready to jump back.

"Sir?"

"I . . . I'm sorry, Miss. Sleeping with my eyes open, I guess. I'm sorry." She didn't believe me. Behind her I saw another woman watching. She must have sent the waitress over. I picked up the check, but I was afraid to try to stand up. I waited until the girl turned and walked away, and then I held the top of the table until I knew my legs would hold me.

I had the boy I'd hired relieve me for the rest of the day, and I walked back to my hotel, slowly, feeling like

an old man. I started the hour-long walk making myself
promises. I would never touch her again, I'd help Lenny
find out the truth about her and do whatever could be
done to cure her, and to get her and Lenny together.
They needed each other, and I had Janet and the
children, and the shop. Everything I had driven for was
either mine, or within sight by now. Everything. She was
a danger to me, nothing else. By the time I got to the
hotel I knew the promises were lies. That as long as I
could get inside that woman's head, I would keep right
on doing it. And now the thought had hit me that I
wanted to be with her physically, just her and me, when
I did it next time. It was a relief finally to admit to myself
that I wanted to seize her body and mind. And I knew
that I wanted everyone else out of her life altogether.
Especially Lenny. Everyone who might be a threat,
everyone who suspected that there was a mystery to be
unraveled. The notebooks would have to be destroyed. If
Karl had known, the knowledge must be destroyed. All
of it. No one to know but me.

I looked on her then as a gift from God or the Devil,
but my gift. From the instant of our first meeting, when
the shock of seeing her had rattled me, right through
that moment, everything had been driving me toward
this realization. I hadn't wanted to see it before. I had
ducked and avoided it. Pretending that she was abhor-
rent to me, making Janet and Lenny shield me from her,
shield her from me. I walked faster and with more
purpose. I had too much to do now to waste time. I had
to learn exactly how to enter her without the panic she
always felt as soon as she knew. And I had to find a way
to make her rid herself of Lenny.

I bought a bottle of bourbon, and some cheese and
crackers. I had to stay in to plan my campaign, make
certain of all the details this time before I touched her. I
knew I would have to be more careful than I had been in
the past. I didn't want to destroy her, or to damage her
in any way. I might have to hurt her at first, just to show

her that she had to obey. That's what always hurt her, having to fight with her. And no more tranquilizers. Karl had been right. She shouldn't have drugs, not she. What else had he learned about her? How deep had his control been? The line from Pete's letter came back to me: "He wound her up each morning. . . ."

The bastard, I thought with hatred. Goddamned bastard.

It was almost five when I got to my room. There was a message from Lenny, to call him at *her* number. I crumpled up the note and flung it across the room. How much of the notebooks had he been able to get through? How much had he told her about what he had found there? I poured a generous drink and tried to think about Lenny and Karl, and all the time I kept seeing her, a tiny, perfectly formed figure, amazingly large dark eyes, doll-like hands. . . .

She would have called Lenny after my . . . visit. I cursed myself for clumsiness. I'd have her in an institution if I wasn't more careful. Had she been able to get back to present after I ran out this time? I realized that that's how I had always left her, in a panic, or in a faint. What if she, in desperation, jumped out a window, or took an overdose of something? I took a long drink and then placed the call. I was shaking again, this time with fear that she was hurt, really hurt.

Lenny answered. "Oh, Eddie. Can you get Weill tonight? I can get in by ten fifteen in the morning. Can you find out if he can see us then?"

I swallowed hard before I could answer. "Sure. He said to call anytime. Someone will be there. Is that all? I mean when I got the message to call you at . . . her house, I was afraid something had happened."

"No. It's all right. Chris has decided to feed me, that's all." There was a false note in his voice. Probably she was nearby, listening. I fought the impulse to go out to her to find out.

"Okay. If I don't call back, assume that it's set up."

"What's wrong with you? You sound hoarse."

"Out in the rain. A bug. I'm catching that mysterious 'it' that's always going around. See you tomorrow."

"Yeah. Take care of yourself. Get a bottle and go to bed."

"Sure, Lenny."

I stared at the phone after hanging up. He was suspicious. I could tell from his voice, from the way he hedged when I asked a direct question. Maybe not simply suspicious. Maybe they actually knew by now. Not that he could prove anything. To whom? Janet? A jury? I laughed and poured another drink, this time mixing it with water. "This man, ladies and gentlemen, entered the mind of this woman at will. . . ."

At breakfast the next morning I realized that I hadn't eaten anything for a couple of days, and still didn't want to then. I had coffee and toast, and left most of the soggy bread on the dish. Lenny met me at the hotel.

"God, Eddie, you'd better get home and go to bed. We can close up the display. You look like hell."

"A bug. I'll be all right. Maybe you could stay if I do decide to take off?"

"Let's close the whole thing. It's just three more days."

"I'll stay," I said. What an ideal set-up that would have been. Him here, me back home, Janet working.

I let Lenny do the talking at Weill's office, and we got a good offer, not as much as we had hoped, but probably more than Weill had planned to make. We ended up saying that our lawyer would go over the contract and be in touch.

"Let's go to your room where we can talk without interruption," Lenny said then, and neither of us mentioned Weill again. A few months ago, B.C., Before Christine, we'd have been arrested for disturbing the peace if we'd had this offer from someone like Weill, and now, we didn't even mention it again.

I lay down on my bed and let Lenny have the only

chair in the room. My head was ringing and aching mildly, and my back and legs were stiff and sore. I didn't give a damn about Lenny's problems then.

Lenny paced. "God, I don't even know where or how to begin this," he said finally. "Back at the beginning of Christine and Karl. She was such a good subject for his experiments that he based much of his research on her alone, using the other two for controls mostly. Then he found out that she was too good, that what she could do was so abnormal that he couldn't base any conclusions on his findings on her. For instance, he trained her to see objects so small that they were too small to fall on the cones and rods in the retina. And he trained her to spot a deviation in a straight line so minute that it needs special equipment to measure. Same with a circle. She can tell the exact place that a circle deviates from sphericity, and again it needs sophisticated instruments to measure it. Stereo acuity. We lose it if the peripheral vision is flattened out, if we don't have the cues. She doesn't lose it. She can see things where there isn't enough light to see them. She can see things that are too far away to see. Same with her color perception. You need a spectrometer and a spectrophotometer to make the same differentiation she can do with a glance."

He stopped and threw himself down in the chair and lighted a cigarette before he continued. "I'm getting pretty well into the notebooks. It's tough going, very technical, in a field I know nothing about. And he knew nothing about physics, and used layman's language, and a sort of shade-tree mechanic's approach with some of the equipment he had to learn to use. Anyway, after a few years, he switched to a second code. He was paranoid about his secrets. A developing psychosis is written down there plain enough even for me to see. He was afraid of her." Lenny put out the cigarette and looked at me. I was watching him, and now I shook my head.

"What do you mean afraid? Her schizophrenia? Was she showing signs of it again?"

"Will you forget that! She's not a schizo! Pretend you look at this room and you see it as it's been all through its history, with everyone who was ever here still here. Suppose you can't stop yourself from straying in time, just the way you stray in space. If you were lost in a hotel like this one and had to knock on doors, or ask people the way to your room, that's being lost in space. Lost in time is worse because no one answers until you find your own time. But those who are in your time see the search, hear your end of it, and wham, you're in a hospital."

I swung my legs over the side of the bed and sat up, but the room was unsteady. I had to support my head on my hands, propped up on my knees. "So why isn't she locked up?"

"Because she learned how to control it most of the time. Maybe a lot of people are born able to see through time and learn as infants to control it, how to tell this present from all the other images that they see. Maybe only a few do it, and most of them never learn control. God knows something drives some children into autism that they never leave. She learned. But in periods of high stress she backslid. If she became overtired, or sick, or under a strain, she couldn't hold the present in sharp enough focus. So they had her in and out of hospitals. And Rudeman became fascinated by her, and began to do his own line of research, using her, and he realized that she was seeing layers of time. Can't you just see it? Him the famous physiological psychologist denying mind from the start, being forced finally to concede that there's something there besides the brain. He struggled. It's all there. He couldn't accept, then he looked for a reasonable cause for her aberrations, finally he knew that she was somehow existing partly in another dimension that opened time just as space is opened to the rest of us." Lenny's sudden laugh was bitter and harsh. "He preferred to think he was going mad, that she was mad. But the scientist in him wouldn't let it rest there. He

devised one experiment after another to disprove her abilities, and only got in deeper and deeper. First understanding, then control. He taught her how to look at *now*. He forced her into photography as part of her therapy, a continuing practice in seeing what is now."

He couldn't see my face. If he had found out that much, he must have learned the rest, I kept thinking. I couldn't tell if he suspected me or not, but if he knew that someone was driving her back into that condition, he would go down the list of names, and sooner or later he would get to me. I knew he would stop there. Too many signs. Too much evidence of my guilt. He'd know. Janet would know. I remembered the toast that *she* had made that night in her house: to the good men. I wanted to laugh, or cry.

"Christ, Eddie, I'm sorry. Here you are as sick as a dog, and I'm going on like a hysterical grandmother."

"I'm not that sick," I said and raised my head to prove it. "It just seemed like as good a way as any to listen. It's a pretty incredible story, you have to admit."

"Yeah, but you ain't heard nothing yet. Chris thinks that Rudeman is haunting her. And why not? If you know you can see the past, where do you draw the line at what is or isn't possible? She's certain that he found a way to come back and enter her mind, and she's having a harder and harder time holding on to the present. She thinks he's having revenge. He always threatened her with a relapse if she didn't cooperate wholly with him in his research."

Lenny's big face registered despair and hopelessness. He spread his hands and said, "After you swallow half a dozen unbelievable details, why stop at one more? But, damn it, I can't take that, and I know something has driven her back to the wall."

I stood up then and looked through the drawer where I had put the bourbon. Then I remembered that it was in the bathroom. When I came back with it, Lenny took the bottle and said, "When did you eat last?"

"I don't remember. Yesterday maybe."

"Yeah, I thought so. I'll have something sent up, then a drink, or you'll pass out."

While we waited I said, "Look at it this way. She sees things that no one else sees. Most people would call that hallucinating. A psychiatrist would call it hallucinating. She thinks her dead husband is haunting her somehow. What in hell are you proposing to do, old buddy?"

Lenny nodded. "I know all that. Did you know that Eric is color blind?" I shook my head. Eric was his middle son. "I didn't know it either until he was tested for it at school. A very sophisticated test that's been devised in the past twenty-five years. Without that test no one would have suspected it ever. You see? I always assumed that he saw things pretty much the way I did. I assume that you see what I see. And there's no way on this earth to demonstrate one way or the other that you do or don't. The mental image you construct and call sight might duplicate mine, or it might not, and it doesn't matter as long as we agree that that thing you're sitting on is a bed. But do you see that as the same bed that I see? I don't know. Let me show you a couple of the easy tests that Karl Rudeman used." He held up a card and flashed it at me. "What color was it?"

I grinned. I had expected to be asked which one it was. "Red," I said. "Red Queen of Hearts."

He turned the card over and I looked at it and nodded, then looked at him. He simply pointed again to the card. It was black. A black Queen of Hearts. I picked it up and studied it. "I see what you mean," I said. I had "seen" it as red.

"Another one," he said. "How many windows are in your house?"

I thought a moment, then said, "Twenty-one."

"How do you know?"

"I just counted them." I was grinning at him and his simple-minded games. But then I started to think, how had I known, how had I counted them? I had visualized

room after room, had counted the windows on the walls that I had drawn up before that inner eye. The bellboy rang and came in with a cart. I tipped him and we sat down to eat sandwiches and drink coffee. "So?" I asked, with my mouth full. "So I visualized the windows. So what does that mean?"

"It means that that's how you remember things. If you had an eidetic memory, you would have seen the walls exactly as they were when you memorized them, and you could have counted the books in your line of vision, read off the titles even. The question is: are you looking into the past? No answer yet. That's what Chris can do. And that's how she sees the past. That clearly. And she sees the anomalies. You see what you expect—a red Queen of Hearts. She sees what is. But, as you say, no psychiatrist would believe it. Rudeman didn't for years, not until he did a lot of checking."

I was wolfing down the sandwiches, while he was still working on the first one. I felt jubilant. He didn't know. She didn't know. Karl haunting her! That was as good a thing for her to think as anything else.

"Okay," I said, pouring more coffee. "I see that she'd have a problem with a psychiatrist. But what's the alternative, if she's as—sick—or bothered as she seems to be?"

"The answer's in the notebooks," Lenny said. "She knows it. She tried to find it at the farmhouse, but it was impossible to work there. And now she's afraid of Rudeman all over again. She believes that somehow she caused his death. Now she has to pay."

The strong waves of guilt I had got from her. But why had he wandered out in the fields barefoot and in pajamas?

"What scares me," Lenny said, "is the slowness of getting through those notes. Bad enough while he was sane, but immeasurably harder as his psychosis developed, for the last seven or eight years. It's like trying to swim in a tar pit. By the end it was bad enough that he

was certifiable, I guess. He knew the contents of those notebooks would invalidate all the work he had done in the past. Chris doesn't want to talk about it, and all I know for sure is what I've been able to dig out of that code he used."

"Psychotic how?"

"Oh, God! I don't know what name they'd put on it. In the beginning he thought she was a puppet that he could manipulate as he chose. Then gradually he became afraid of her, Chris. Insanely jealous, mad with fear that she'd leave him, terrified that someone would find out about her capabilities and begin to suspect that there was more. Just batty."

"So what do you intend to do?"

"That's what I came up here to talk to you about. I'm going to marry her." I jerked my head around to stare at him in disbelief. He smiled fleetingly. "Yeah, it's like that. Not until next year sometime. But I'm taking her on a long, long trip, starting as soon as we can get the books we'll need ready. That's why I want to wrap up a deal with Weill as fast as we can. I'll need my share. We can handle the shop however you want—keep my bench waiting, or buy me out. Whatever."

I kept on staring at him, feeling very stupid. "What books?" I asked finally, not wanting to know, but to keep him talking long enough for me to try to understand what it would mean to me.

"Rudeman used his library shelves as keys throughout. Things like one—eleven—two ninety-eight—three —six. Top row, eleventh book, page two ninety-eight, line three, word six. First three letters correspond to ABC and so on. He'd use that for a while, then switch to another book. Chris memorized those shelves, so she can find the key books. Stumbled onto it a couple of years ago. That's why she dragged all of his books with her when she ducked out of that house. She just didn't have time to go through the notebooks to sort out the ones he had used."

"Lenny, are you sure? Isn't it just the sick-bird syndrome? I mean, my God, maybe she really *is* crazy! A lot of beautiful, charming, talented people are."

"No. She isn't. Rudeman would have known after all those years. He wanted her to be, but he couldn't convince himself in the slightest that she was." He stood up. "I didn't expect you to believe me. I would have been disappointed in you if you had. But I had to get it out, get some of this stuff said. Let you know you'll have the shop to yourself for a year or so."

"What are you going to do now?"

"Go home. Move in the Donlevy house. She's on tranquilizers, and they make it awfully hard to hold on to the present. She keeps wandering back and forth. It'll take a week to get things ready to leave." He mock-cuffed me and said, "Don't look so worried. I know what I'm doing."

When he was gone I wished that he had a real inkling of what he was doing, and I knew that he would never know. I thought about that line that everyone has that he can't cross, no matter what the evidence, unless there is an inner revelatory experience. Rudeman couldn't believe she looked into the past, until he experienced it through her. Then he drew the line at possession, until it was proven again, and with its proof he had come to doubt his own sanity. Lenny could accept the research that proved she could see the past, but no farther. Whatever Rudeman had said about possession he had written off as insanity. And I had blundered in and swallowed the whole thing without reservation, through experience, firsthand experience. I tried to think in what ways I was like Rudeman, making it possible for me to do what he had done, wondering why Lenny couldn't do it, why others hadn't. My gift. Like my fingerprints were mine alone. I gave Lenny ten minutes to make sure that he really was gone, then I looked in on her. I said it to myself that way, Think I'll look in on her now.

Met by a wave of hatred stronger than anything I'd ever experienced. Resistance. Determination not to be taken again. Thoughts: not going crazy. You're real and evil. Die! Damn you, die! I killed you once! How many times! *Die!*

I drew back, but not all the way. She thought she was winning. She conjured a vision of a man in pajamas, orange and black stripes, walking, a pain in the chest, harder and harder, gasping for air. . . . I clutched the arms of the chair and said, "No! Stop thinking. No more!" The pain returned, and this time I was falling, falling. . . . I had to get out. Get away from her. The witch, bitch, which witch bitch. Falling. Pain. I couldn't get loose. Falling. Out the window, over the rail, backward, seeing the ground . . . She screamed and let go.

I lay back in the chair, trying to catch my breath, trying to forget the pain in my chest, my shoulder, my left arm. I didn't have a heart condition. Perfectly all right. Medical exam just last year. Perfectly all right. I flexed the fingers in my hand, and slowly raised the arm, afraid the pain would return with movement.

Bitch, I thought. The goddamn bitch. She hadn't taken the tranquilizer, she had been waiting, steeled against me, ready to attack. Treacherous bitch. I pushed myself from the chair and stood up, and saw myself in the mirror. Grey. Aged. Terrified. I closed my eyes and said again, "Bitch!"

Was she panting also, like a fighter between rounds? If I went again now, would she be able to attack again so soon? I knew I wouldn't try. The pain had been too real.

I looked at my watch then and nearly fell down again. An hour and a half? I held it to my ear, and shook it hard. An hour and a half! Shakily I called Weill's office and told Hendrickson that he could have the machine tool picked up any time. I was going home.

There wasn't much else there, nothing that I couldn't get to the car alone. And by five I was on the highway. An hour and a half, I kept thinking. Where? Doing what?

She would kill me, I thought over and over. Just like she killed her husband. The notebooks, I had to get them myself. I couldn't let Lenny take them away. Rudeman must have discovered too late that she had power too. But he must have suspected before the end. His psychosis. The new code, afraid she had learned the old one. He must have learned about this. He had kept her ten years before she killed him. It would be in the notebooks. I drove too fast, and got home in six hours. And not until the car squealed to a stop in the driveway did I even think about what I would tell Lenny or Janet. But I didn't have to tell her anything. She took one look at my face and cried, "Oh, my God!" And she pulled me from the car and got me inside and into bed somehow, without any help from me, but without hindrance either. And I fell asleep.

I woke up when Janet did to get the kids off to school. "Are you better? I called Dr. Lessing last night, and he said to bring you in this morning."

"I'm better," I said wearily. I felt like I was coming out of a long drugged sleep, with memories hazy and incomplete. "I need to sleep and have orange juice, and that's about it. No need for you to stay home." She said she'd see about that, and she went out to get Rusty up, and to find Laura's red scarf. I hadn't seen them for almost a week, hadn't even thought of them. They would expect presents. They always expected presents. When Janet came back in fifteen minutes, I convinced her that I really was all right, and finally she agreed to go on to work. She'd call at noon.

I had breakfast. I showered and dressed. And smoked three cigarettes. And convinced myself that I wasn't sick at all. And then I walked over to Christine's house.

Lenny met me at the door. "What the hell are you doing up and out? Janet said you came in sick as a dog last night." He gave me more coffee. At the kitchen table.

"I kept thinking about what you were saying about

her." I indicated the rest of the house. "And I was sick, feverish, and decided I couldn't do anything else in Chicago. So I came home. Anything I can do to help?"

Lenny looked like he wanted to hug me, but he said merely, "Yeah, I can use some help."

"Tell me what to do."

"Just stick around until Chris wakes up. I gave her a sleeping pill last night. Should be wearing off soon. What I've been doing is going down the notebooks line by line and every time he used another book for his key, Chris visualizes the shelf and finds it there. Then we find that book in the boxes. And I go on to the next one. While she rests, or is busy with her work, I find the key words in the books and decode a line or two to make sure. Rather not lug that whole library with us if I can avoid it."

I was watching him as if he were a stranger. I was thinking of him as a stranger. I had no definite plan worked out, just a direction. *She* had to get rid of him. Before he learned any more from the notebooks.

And her. What did she know? I knew I had to find out without any more delay. I tried to reach her and found a cottony foggy world. The sleeping pill. I tried to jar her awake, and got glimpses of a nightmare world of grey concrete expanses. A hall, the grey of the floor exactly matched the grey of the walls and ceiling. The joints lost their squareness ahead of me, and the hallway became a tube that grew narrower and narrower and finally was only a point. I was running toward the point at a breakneck speed.

You're not Karl! Who are you? I pulled out. What if she brought the pain again? The pseudo heart attack? I was shaking.

"Jesus, Eddie, you should be in bed." Lenny put his hand on my forehead. "Come on, I'll take you home."

I shook my head. "I'm okay. Just get a chill now and then. How about the couch here? At least I'll be handy when she gets up."

He installed me in the study on the deep green couch,

with an Indian throw over me. I drifted pleasantly for a while. Then, *Get out! Who are you?—I'll never get out again. Karl knew, didn't he? I'll finish what he started. You can't hurt me the way you hurt him. I'm too strong for you. We'll go away, you and me.* I laughed, and laughing pulled away. At the same instant I heard her scream.

I sat up and waited. Lenny brought her down in a few minutes. I didn't join them in the kitchen. I watched and listened through her, and she was so agitated now that she wasn't even aware of my presence. I was getting that good at it.

"Listen, Lenny, and then leave me alone. I thought it was Karl, but it isn't. I don't know who it is. He can get inside my mind. I don't know how. I know he's there, and he makes me do things, crazy things. He'll use me, just like Karl did all those years. I can't help myself. And night after night, day after day, whatever he wants me to do, wherever he wants me to go . . ." She was weeping and her talk was beginning to break up into incoherent snatches of half-formed thoughts.

"Chris! Stop that! Your husband was crazy! He thought he could possess you. That's insane! And he half convinced you that he could do it. But God damn it, he's dead! No one else can touch you. I won't let anyone near you."

"He doesn't have to be near me. All these weeks . . . He's been in and out, watching, listening to us go over the notebooks. He knows what's in them now. I . . . He won't stop now. And if he says I have to go with him, I'll have to."

Her voice went curiously flat and lifeless. She was seeing again that tube that ended in a point, and suddenly she longed to be on it, heading toward that point. "I'd rather die now," she said.

Lenny's big face twisted with pain. "Chris, please, trust me. I won't let anyone near you. I promise. Let me help you, Chris. Please. Don't force me out now."

"It won't make any difference. You don't understand. If he makes me go with him, I can't fight it."

But she could. I didn't know if my thoughts reminded her of the heart attack, or if she would have thought of it herself. Karl sitting in her room, watching her with a smile on his face. "You will turn them down, of course, my dear. You can't travel to Africa alone."

"No, I won't turn them down! I want to take this assignment. . . ." Slipping, blurring images, fear of being alone, of not being able to keep the world in focus. Fear of falling through the universe, to a time where there was nothing, falling forever. . . . Staring at the rejection of the offer in her own handwriting. Karl's face, sad, but determined.

"You really don't want to travel without me, my dear. It wouldn't be safe for you, you know."

And later, waking up from dreamless sleep. Knowing she had to get up, to go down the hall to his room, where he was waiting for her. *No! It's over! Leave me alone.* Swinging her legs over the side of the bed, standing up, *NO! I HATE YOU! Your soft fat hands! You make me feel dirty! Why don't you die! Have a heart attack and die.*

Fighting it to the door, dragging herself unwillingly to the door, fighting against the impulse, despising him and even more herself. He was forcing her up flights of stairs, without rails, straight down for miles and miles, and he was at her side, forcing each step. She pushed him, and he screamed. Then he was there again, and she pushed again. And again. Then he was running, and she, clinging to the doorknob in her bedroom, she was running too, pushing him off the steps as fast as he managed to climb back on, and he stumbled and fell and now she knew he would fall forever, even as she fell sometimes. Swirling into darkness with pain and terror for company. She slipped to the floor, and awakened there much later knowing only that something was gone from her life. That she felt curiously free and empty and unafraid.

I lay back down and stared at the ceiling. I could hear her footsteps recede up the stairs, across the hall to her room. Lenny's heavy tread returned and there was the

sound of measured pacing. Soon, I thought. Soon it would end. And after today, after she recovered from the next few hours . . . She would have to remain nearby, here in this house as long as possible. Above me she was starting to dress. I was there. She didn't doubt a presence haunting her. Nor did she question that he could force her to go away with him if he chose.

"Who?" she whispered, standing still with her eyes closed. She imagined the suppressed fury on Lenny's big face, the pulse in his temple that beat like a primitive drum summoning him from this time back to a time when he would have killed without a thought anyone who threatened his woman. I laughed and forced his face to dissolve and run like a painting on fire.

Suddenly I was jerked from my concentration by the sound of Janet's voice. "Where is he? How is he?"

"He's sleeping in the study. Feverish, but not bad." Lenny's reassuring voice.

Janet came into the study and sat on the couch and felt my face. "Honey, I was scared to death. I called and called and no answer. I was afraid you'd passed out or something. Let me take you over to Dr. Lessing."

"Get out," I said without opening my eyes. "Just get out and leave me alone." I tried to find *her*, and couldn't. I was afraid to give it too much attention with Janet right there.

"I can't just leave you like this. I've never seen you like this before. You need a doctor."

"Get out of here! When I need you or want you I'll be in touch. Just get the hell away from me now."

"Eddie!"

"For God's sake, Janet, can't you leave me alone? I've got a virus, a bug. I feel rotten, but not sick, not sick enough for a doctor. I just want to be left alone."

"No. It's more serious than that. Don't you think I know you better than that? It's been coming on for weeks. Little things, then bigger things, now this. You have to see a doctor, Eddie. Please."

Wearily I sat up and stared at her and wondered how

I'd ever found her attractive or desirable. Freckled, thin, sharp features, razorlike bones . . . I turned away and said, "Get lost, Janet. Beat it. Yeah, it started a long time ago, but it takes a club over the head, doesn't it?"

"What do you mean?"

"Just what you think I mean. I'm sick. I'm tired. I want to be alone. For a long time. Tonight. Tomorrow night. Next week. Next month. Just get out of here and leave me alone. I'll pick up some things later on after you've gone to work."

"I'm going to call Dr. Lessing."

I looked at her and hoped I wouldn't have to hit her. I didn't want to hurt her, too. Her freckles stood out in relief against the dead white of her skin. I closed my eyes. "I won't see him. Or anyone else. Not now. Maybe tomorrow. Just leave me alone for now. I have to sleep."

She stood up and backed away. She had seen. She knew that I'd hit her if she didn't get out. At the door she stopped, and the helplessness in her voice made me want to throw something at her. "Eddie? Will you stay here for the next hour?"

So she could bring in her men in white. I laughed and sat up. "I had planned to, but I guess I'd better plan again. I'll be in touch."

She left then. I could hear her voice and Lenny's from the kitchen, but I didn't try to make out their words. A clock chimed twelve. I wanted to go out there and throw Janet out. I didn't want her around for the next half hour or so. I heard the back door, then the sound of a motor, and I sighed in relief.

I went to the kitchen and got coffee and stood at the window watching snow fall.

Lenny joined me. "Janet says you had a fight."

"Yeah. I was rough on her. Sickness brings out her mother-hen instincts, and I can't stand being fussed at. What was wrong with Christine?"

"A dream." He stared at the snow. "Supposed to get a couple of inches by night, I think. Won't stick long. Ground isn't cold enough yet."

"Lenny, for God's sake quit kidding yourself. She's sick. She needs professional help."

"She thinks—she's certain that he learned enough about her to put an end to this so-called illness. She's desperately afraid of a relapse. Hospitalization, shock therapy . . ."

"What if *you* are causing her present condition? Isn't it suggestive? Her husband, now you. It's a sexual fantasy. By making her reach a decision about you, you might push her off the deep end irreversibly."

He looked shocked. "That's crazy."

"Exactly. Lenny, these things are too dangerous for a well-meaning but non-professional man to toy with. You might destroy her. . . ."

"If she was crazy you'd be making good points," Lenny said distinctly. "She isn't."

I finished my coffee. *A doctor. Shots, pills, all yesterday and last years and decades ago. Questions. Lost forever and forever falling. Through all the yesterdays. Lenny wants to get a doctor for you. A psychiatrist. You have to get him out of here now. Immediately. Even if it kills him.*

She resisted the idea. She kept trying to visualize his face, and I wouldn't let it take shape. Instead I drew out of her memories of the institutions she'd been in.

Lenny's voice startled me, and I left her.

"I don't think it's such a good idea for you to be here when she comes down. She knows you think she's psycho."

I put down my cup. "Whatever you say."

She came into the kitchen then. She was deathly pale. She had a gun in her hand. I stared at it. "Where . . . ?"

She looked at it too, looked at it in a puzzled manner. "I had it in my car when I came here," she said. "I found it when I was unpacking and I put it upstairs in my room. I just remembered."

"Give it to me," Lenny said. He held out his hand and she put the small automatic in it.

I sighed my relief. That was the last thing I wanted her to do. She'd be locked up the rest of her life. Now if I

could make her drive him out, maybe he'd use it
himself.

Lenny kept his hand in his pocket, over the gun. "Why
were you thinking of guns right now? Where was this?"

"In my train case. I told you . . ." She glanced at me
and I turned my back to stare at the snow again. I was
watching my own back then, and seeing Lenny's face
and the kitchen that I was keeping in focus only through
great effort. "I told you," she said again. "If he makes
me go back with him, I'll have no choice." I made her
add, "The only way I escaped from Karl was through his
death."

She shuddered, and an image of Karl's face swam
before her eyes. It was contorted with pain and fear. It
was replaced by another face, Lenny's, also contorted
by pain and fear. And the image of a hospital ward, and a
doctor. And I watched his face change and become my
own face. The image dimmed and blurred as I tried to
force it away, and she fought to retain it. The concrete
corridor was there. She forced the image of a man
backward through the corridor, grey walls and ceiling
and floor all one, no up and no down, just the cylinder
that was growing smaller and smaller. I tried to pull
away, and again there was a duel as she fought to keep
the imagery. Cliffs, I thought. Crumbling edges, falling
. . . Hospital, shots, electroshock . . .

"Chris, what is it?" Lenny's voice, as if from another
world, faint, almost unrecognizable.

"I don't know. Just hold me. Please."

Cliffs . . . Exploding pain in my chest suddenly. Burning pain in my shoulder, my arm. Darkness. Losing her,
finding her again. Losing . . .

"You!" Her voice coarse, harsh with disbelief.

I turned from the window clutching my chest. The
room was spinning and there was nothing to hold on to.
Let go. They'll lock you up. Pain.

"Eddie!"

"You!" she said again, incredulously.

Get the gun back! Lenny. No more pretense now. My hand found something to hold, and the room steadied. Feeling of falling, but knowledge of standing perfectly still, fighting against the nausea, the pain. *Get the gun. Reach in his pocket and take it out*. We, she and I, were in that other place where the grey corridor stretched endlessly. We had time because there was no time. She backed a step away from Lenny, and I forced her to move closer again, seeing the beads of sweat on her forehead, the trembling in her hands. From somewhere else I could hear Lenny's voice, but I couldn't hear the words now. GET THE GUN!

"Lenny, get out! Leave. Go away fast. He'll kill you!" Her voice came from that other place, but the words were echoed up and down the corridor.

You and I. I'll take care of you. I won't let anyone hurt you.

Lenny's hands on me, trying to force me to a chair. Seeing myself sprawled across the table unconscious. *"No!"* I tried to make her fall down an elevator shaft, and saw even clearer my own figure across the table. I tried to remember how it felt to fall in an uncontrollable plunge, and nothing came. She had to faint. Something could be salvaged even now, if only she would faint, or have hysterics, or something, I couldn't break out, pull away. She was holding the back of a chair with both hands, holding so hard her muscles hurt. I saw her grasp tighten and felt the pain erupt again, this time blacking out everything momentarily. Lenny . . . I couldn't make her move. I slipped my hand into his pocket then and my fingers felt the metal, warm from the close pocket. I pulled it out and aimed it at Lenny. I was seeing his face from a strange angle, her angle. A cross-section of his face. A Dali painting of fear and shock. She was beating on me and I closed my other hand over her wrist, a child's wrist. Laura's wrist. Back in that timeless corridor. *Why didn't you look into the future too? Why just the past?*

He said I did. I repressed it. Too frightening. The image of the man sprawled across the table, clearer, detailed. Real.

Absolute terror then. Hers. Everything shifting, spinning away, resolving into strange shapes, displaced items of furniture, strange people moving about. Intolerable pain as she lashed out in desperation to find her way through the maze of time. And I was outside again.

I tried to go into her and couldn't. I could see her, wide-eyed, catatonic, and couldn't reach her at all. It was as if the wall that had been breached had been mended now, and once again kept me and all others outside. I didn't know how I had gone through it before. I didn't even know if I had.

I heard the gun hit the floor before I realized that I had dropped it. I felt the table under my cheek before I realized that I had collapsed and was lying across it. I heard their voices, and I knew that she had found her way back, but I couldn't see them. For the moment I was free of the pain. Almost uninterested in the figure slumped across the table.

"You'd better get an ambulance," she said. I marveled at the calm self-assurance in her voice. What had she seen while she had stood unmoving, rigid? She touched my forehead with fingers that were cool and steady.

"Was it real?" I whispered. "Any of it?"

"You'll never know, will you?" I didn't know if she said the words aloud or not. I listened to their voices drifting in and out of consciousness while we waited for the ambulance. Was it real? I kept coming back to that.

Was what real?

Anything.

THE TOR DOUBLES

Two complete short science fiction novels in one volume!

☐ 53362-3 A MEETING WITH MEDUSA by Arthur C. Clarke and $2.95
   55967-3 GREEN MARS by Kim Stanley Robinson   Canada $3.95

☐ 55971-1 HARDFOUGHT by Greg Bear and $2.95
   55951-7 CASCADE POINT by Timothy Zahn   Canada $3.95

☐ 55952-5 BORN WITH THE DEAD by Robert Silverberg and $2.95
   55953-3 THE SALIVA TREE by Brian W. Aldiss   Canada $3.95

☐ 55956-8 TANGO CHARLIE AND FOXTROT ROMEO $2.95
   55957-6 by John Varley and   Canada $3.95
            THE STAR PIT by Samuel R. Delany

☐ 55958-4 NO TRUCE WITH KINGS by Poul Anderson and $2.95
   55954-1 SHIP OF SHADOWS by Fritz Leiber   Canada $3.95

☐ 55963-0 ENEMY MINE by Barry B. Longyear and $2.95
   54302-5 ANOTHER ORPHAN by John Kessel   Canada $3.95

☐ 54554-0 SCREWTOP by Vonda N. McIntyre and $2.95
   55959-2 THE GIRL WHO WAS PLUGGED IN   Canada $3.95
            by James Tiptree, Jr.

Buy them at your local bookstore or use this handy coupon:
Clip and mail this page with your order.

Publishers Book and Audio Mailing Service
P.O. Box 120159, Staten Island, NY 10312-0004

Please send me the book(s) I have checked above. I am enclosing $_____
(please add $1.25 for the first book, and $.25 for each additional book to
cover postage and handling. Send check or money order only—no CODs.)

Name _____

Address _____

City _____ State/Zip _____

Please allow six weeks for delivery. Prices subject to change without notice.